Life Without Hero's

Lasting Life Scars

Donald D. Conley, Sr.

Order this book online at www.trafford.com
or email orders@trafford.com

Most Trafford titles are also available at major online book retailers.

Print information available on the last page.

ISBN: 978-1-6987-0540-8 (sc)
ISBN: 978-1-6987-0541-5 (e)

Trafford rev. 01/19/2021

Trafford
PUBLISHING www.trafford.com
North America & international
toll-free: 844-688-6899 (USA & Canada)
fax: 812 355 4082

CONTENTS

Being able to let go of mental scars inflicted during the formative years of life is not always as simple as it may sound to most Those of whom at least claim to have taken charge of those scars and put them to positive efforts towards living a better life, I commend.

On the other hand there are people who are of a different nature that will not allow them to even feel a compulsion to overlook an injustice, be it consciously or unconsciously they carry these old emotional life war wounds with them.

Regardless of the road one chooses in life, knowing where one has been emotionally, regardless of how much time has passed still there will always be an emotional blemish from those scars. The choice we make after that still can only rest with one's self...

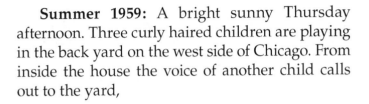

Summer 1959: A bright sunny Thursday afternoon. Three curly haired children are playing in the back yard on the west side of Chicago. From inside the house the voice of another child calls out to the yard,

"Johnny, daddy want's you!" Obediently the nine year old boy walks quickly inside the house, not allowing his eyes enough time to adjust to the darkness as he walked into his father's bedroom, where he lay just getting home from his second job

"Boy what you out there doing making your sister cry!" but before any reply could be uttered Stars filled the dark room and pain from a vicious open hand slap across his face and a-

"Now get on out of here and don't let me hear nothing else out of you!" No need to attempt an explanation. Feeling his way out of the room reeling from the impact of the assault, like a blind man without a cane. I suppose any other child would have felt admonished, instead it was a feeling of an unjust assault that needed to be returned in the same fashion.

His father always kept a gun, a Smith & Wesson 38. Revolver and Johnny knew where he kept it. The bed room was dark as his father lay asleep after working the graveyard shift at Joliet State prison. Johnny feeling his way in the dark takes the gun out of the bottom drawer then quietly walks over to where his father lay sleeping and just as he aims the gun at the sleeping parent, suddenly the cries of his infant baby sister in her nearby crib stops him in the process and he put the gun away. Had his father awaken Johnny would have shot him.

The following week as part of the summer program Saint Matthews was having an Alter Boy practice for new servers The Priest is talking to Johnny out on the steps of the church

"Now you're never going be able serve the lord unless you get serious" he said with an Irish accent.

There was something about that priest that did not seem right. He always reeked of wine and stale cigarettes, along with being a bit too touchy feely. His twin brother Tommy along with another Hispanic boy were also there on the church steps practicing and were all following the instructions of the priest like they were Robots

Directly across the street from the church there was a Public School and the public school kids were accustom to seeing boys out on the steps with the priest doing their ritual for whatever reason they were doing it

After the brief discussion with the father, Johnny wanders off near the corner where he is joined by two cute older girls near the bus stop. Leaning on the pole as one immediately runs her right hand through his curly hair, while the other one places her arm around his shoulder and asks,

"What ya'll doin?"

"Alter Boy practice"

"You gone be one?"

"Don't look like it" Johnny replies and one girl suggest,

"Then come on and walk us home" Without further discussion Johnny walks away with both girls holding on to each arm.

Johnny did not have a single thought regarding "Territory" belonging to the Public School Kids and the long way around to the school belonged to the Catholic School kids.

With the two girls at his side the young boy walks directly into a group of older public school boys. They stare menacingly at him but before anyone can say anything, both girls speak saying,

"Ya'll can just get on with all that cause, this our Lil Man" and from that day forward he was protected from the public school gangs by girls who too were in their own gang, so there was mutual respect. Considered as their mascot the girls would take care of him in ways that made him feel like he was worth something.

As the weeks followed and Johnny would always take the direct route to school, instead of taking the long way around, his brothers and sisters thought he had lost his mind, not knowing that he had very good protection. Johnny's twin told their mother what the priest had told his brother about not making the grade to pass the test to be an Alter Boy and even though his mother threatened a severe beating should he not make it, still he had it in his mind that he would not and he did not.

1961, 5 years later Easter Sunday Morning Mass at St. Matthews Catholic church where a large crowd of church goers have gathered all neatly dressed in their ultimate best. Including Johnny and his family of seven Three boys and four girls with the exception of his father

The family all band together as his mother bends to adjust his tie so she can scold him

"I don't know why you can't be like your brother

He made alter boy, but no! you couldn't", just as his twin Tommy comes running up wearing the Alter Boy Gown,

"Momma Momma!" His mother is still bending down in front of Johnny and says,

"Now you see how good your brother looks in his robe!" but the boy has his mind elsewhere not hearing a word his mother said, until she pulls his right ear then slaps him

"Pay attention when I talk to you boy!" Tommy shares his news with his mother

"Momma, the father asked me if I would be his number one Alter Boy Can I Momma Can I?" He is clearly excited and proud of his pending appointment

"You most certainly can" she approves then returns her attention to Johnny,

"I don't know why you got to be so hard headed!" all the while he has a look on his face as if to say

"I know something about the priest that you don't know" smiling to himself

After church was over the procession of mother and seven children made the short walk back to the two story brick home. Easter Sunday dinner and the entire family is seated around the dining room table including their father while mother is bustling about in and out of the kitchen serving the dinner.

His father stood at the head of the table carved the turkey while finishing his second tall glass of Whiskey under the watchful eye

Of their mother,

"Now Ed, you know you got to go to work tonight,

So I don't know why you sitting' up drinking like that!"

"Alright now Sue, I been working all week an' I may just

Go around to the pool hall for a bit" She looks at her husband with defiance in her eyes saying,

"Okay" she chimed sarcastically, "But I'm gone send that boy around there if you stay too long!" while he empties his glass and walks out of the front door.

It was close to eleven p.m. when his mother entered the bedroom he shared with his other two brothers telling him to go to the pool hall and tell his father it's time to come home. Johnny actually enjoyed having to go out late at night when it was cold because, he was born with asthma and the old steam heaters in the Chicago homes made it feel as if you were in the middle of a sweltering forest, but outside he could breath even run for long periods of time without getting tired or winded., which is what he did this night. He ran all the way.

The pool hall was located on Lake Street just past Kedsie The sound of Junior Wells bellowing his song Up In Here from the juke box mixed in the cold night air along with the ground shaking sounds of the L Train overhead passing by

As Johnny enters the crowded smoke filled room, loud voices, some laughing, some shouting as he moves slowly closer inside searching for his father when suddenly two clear explosions from a gun at the back of the room creating panic and a stampede. A visible cloud of gun smoke still hangs in the air as the adults run out in fear almost knocking the young boy down. Moments later he watches his father walk briskly out of the building without seeing his son.

Instead of following his father home he went to the back of the pool hall to see a man face down with his head in a pool of blood. At the sight of the motionless man on the floor along with the way everyone except his father ran in fear and even appeared to be concealing something inside his coat pocket it became obvious to Johnny what had happened and who did it

He didn't run back home he walked thinking about what he just saw even questioning if it was real. By the time he made it back home his father was sitting on the side of the bed taking off his socks when he heard to front door open and he called out

"Who the hell is that coming in here at this hour of the night!" Quickly Johnny steps to the bedroom door

"It's me I just got back from-"cut off by his father

"Just make sure that front door is locked, then get upstairs and go to bed" Without comment he complies and scampers upstairs to his room

A few days later Johnny and Tommy are at the neighborhood corner store at the counter an overweight Italian boy around their age behind the counter waits on them. He pushes two small brown paper bags of candy towards them Tommy pays and accepts the change

Once outside walking home Johnny asks his brother,

"Where you get this money from?"

"I saved it" Tommy answers, "I get an allowance remember. You don't because your grades are bad" Walking side by side Tommy reflects,

"You been having money all week long. How you get it?" chewing on a candy bar Johnny reports

"These two girls from the public school across the street, they give me money all the time"

"Yeah right!" Tommy declares in disbelief,

"What, You ask them for it?"

"Nope!" Johnny replies

No! Then why they do that?"

"Because they like me and they older than me"

"So why they like you?"

"I don't know but it's alright with me as long as I can

Keep me a sack of candy" Laughing together as they walk back home

Tommy entered the house first to observe his mother pacing around in the dining room scolding, not talking to anyone else but clearly upset Johnny walks in behind his brother who stands frozen near the dining room table where an open woman's purse sits on top of it

"Where have you two been!" she inquires angrily not waiting for an answer

"And what's in those bags?" Tommy is clearly nervous as he holds up his bag for her to see

"It's some candy we got from the store"

"Well" Mother speaks sternly, "Somebody been in my purse!"

Tommy is clearly nervous while Johnny is standing beside him but still eating his own candy when suddenly Tommy blurts out

"I'm sorry momma"

She placed both hands on her hips staring with piercing eyes leaning slightly forward

"You ungrateful fool and I bet that bastard Johnny put you up to it" She then walked to the hall closet and removes a wire coat hanger, twists it with both hands before she begins to beat Johnny with vicious lashes that rip and cut the flesh on his arms while Tommy cowers in a corner crying as though he is the one being beaten. And when she finished with Johnny she only promised his brother a beating.

Berkeley, California. 1965:

The move from Chicago to California came as a total surprise. There was no discussion or suggestions of there being any type of moving to another State practically on the other side of the Country. Not even having the chance to grasp what was really going on. How long were we going to be in California and when would we be coming back.

Slowly but surely the reality sank in that there would be no going back

Burbank Junior high was in Berkeley, Ca. During the history class when Johnny was asked by the teacher to pass out the text books, which he obliged. With a stack of books cradled in his left arm, he slowly walks down each isle placing a book on the occupied desk.

As he places a book on the desk of a boy to his right and passes him the boy slides his book off the desk and it hits the floor, he speaks

"Say man, you dropped my book"

Johnny knew that he had not but purely for the sake of being civil he picked up the book and placed it back on the desk only for the boy to slide it to the floor again,

"Say man my book!" The boy speaks once more

"Pick it up yourself" Johnny said as he continued on passing out the books all the while listening to everything going on behind him, so when his would-be assailant moved and rustled about he met with a left hand to his jaw and the fight was on Johnny and the boy square off but the boy attempts to wrestle but is met with a right cross until another boy grabs Johnny from the back making it two against one

The class room is in total chaos as Johnny has been more than what the two boys had expected. Boys and girls alike are all out of their seats with the teacher as the referee attempting to break it up. The taller boy is still holding on to Johnny when he ejects himself and hits the boy in the jaw

"I saw that mister!" The teacher said to Johnny, "Now you march yourself up to the vice Principals office and you two follow me as well"

The very first image to enter his mind was an old looking Dennis The Menace when he looked at the tall slender brown haired man speaking

"I'm going to need to see both of your parents

Before I can allow you back in school"

Johnny is standing in front of his desk as he is talking

"You haven't been here long at Burbank have you?"

"No, we just moved here from Chicago"

"We? Explain we" he asks in a calm soft tone of voice

"My mother and nine sisters an brothers" The VP gets up from behind his desk to walk around and take a seat on the desks corner and he asks

"Where is your father?"

"He had to stay back in Chicago to sell our old house,

Then he's coming out here with us"

"I see" the man speaks as if analyzing everything being said while Johnny is still standing in front of him

"Are you sure you didn't get hurt"

"No! I mean yeah I'm sure"

"Alright then, I'm going to have a pass issued allowing

You to go home Have your mother to call me and I'll

Do what I can to get to the bottom of this You're not

In any serious trouble so don't worry"

Expressionless Johnny turns and walks out of the office figuring there really was nothing left to say about anything while the issue with his mother would turn out to be something entirely unexpected.

That same evening Johnny is in the kitchen where his mother is scolding him as she is holding a butcher knife in her right hand as if she is going to strike him with it, yet he stands there. She looks into his eyes then sets the knife on the counter and attempts to hit him, but he catches her by the wrist before she can deliver the blow he defends

"I told you they jumped on me! I was just protecting

Myself so what you trying to hit me for"

"How dare you raise your hand to me!" snatching her arm from his grip when he tells his mother

"No! We not doing that no more that's all

Over with"

"I'm calling your daddy and he gone kill you

When he get here" Eight of the children are there seated around the room having witnessed the entire incident all except his older brother who is on his way in from football practice. When he arrives his mother tells him how Johnny grabbed pushed and shoved her bruising her wrist

Johnny is at the back of the house where the boys all share a room when his brother enters in a rage

"Say man why is MOTHER SO UPSET!" Johnny raises his hands as he says

"Hold up! If you even try to lay hands on me I'll

Cut you every way but loose" as he opens a Switch Blade knife with one flick of his right thumb causing his brother to stumble in retreat

"Get your facts straight before you get your ass checked!" looking into the older boys eyes causing him to turn back around and storm out of the room and house

His mother just knew she would be able to persuade her oldest son to invoke her wrath on his brother but instead he turned and ran which meant a severe almost death punishment would be coming from his father once he arrived from Chicago.

The atmosphere there in the house was uncomfortable so Johnny decided to take advantage of his newly established position in the home He walked outside got on the San Pablo street bus and rode all the way to Mac Author Boulevard in Oakland. From school he had heard that this was the street where all of the real Hustlers and Players gathered from around the Bay and he wanted to see it.

From the window of the bus he was making mental notes and watching where he was going The city of Berkeley seemed more like being out in the country, until you got close to University avenue As the city of Oakland drew closer the scenery seemed to come alive. Long sleek Cadillacs and Lincoln Continental's right hand drive classic Rolls Royce and Mercedes cruising down the streets along with elegantly dressed occupants.

Having been living in Berkeley going on three months, his mother decided she did not like the house and requested that his father send additional funds so she could secure a larger home. With the help of her sister-in-law she found another home in the city of North Oakland

A very nice spacious four bedroom with basement large back yard and three car garage He always thought of his father as quite remarkable yet he could not understand the hold his mother seem to have over him. He was the one who worked two jobs, while all she did was bark orders and claimed to have worked around the house all day

His mother had to enroll her brood in a different school district. The younger children attended catholic school, while the older went to public high schools.

The day his father arrived to California was a joyous event. Everyone was excited. He was towing another car he had bought in Chicago for the oldest son who was soon to be graduating from high school. He had both cars loaded with clothes toys they left in the old house Everyone was clamoring all over him like frisky puppies glad to see the master

Everyone with the exception of Johnny who stood back and away though his father had his eyes on him the moment he pulled into the back yard They even passed words

"How you doing boy?

"Go over there and help your brothers and

Sisters unload those cars" with nothing more than a nod the young boy takes off to do as he was told.

In the days and weeks to follow it was his mission to avoid his father by all means possible which really wasn't all that difficult since his main objective at this point was to find a job in order to sustain his family. The majority of the money from the property sold in Chicago was virtually all gone, so it was the Race Track for many months until he landed a more substantial paying job in San Francisco many months later. From the stories that were told about his Grandfather Jesse, he was a violent man a gambler a womanizer and people all over and throughout Baton Rouge feared him while his mother had a deep seeded hatred for Her father in law whom she totally despised always angrily prophesizing that Johnny was going to be no good just like Jesse Knowing that she did not care for his Grandfather only encouraged the young boy to be just like him He had been murdered long before Johnny was born, shot in the back as he was entering into a Saloon by three men who had gone by his home looking for him but his wife told them where he had gone and they got there just as he did then shot him multiple times in the back

The one photograph Johnny had seen of his grandfather was taken during the 1920's poor quality black and white showing a man with a thick mustache The one thing he found most appealing about his late grandfather was how he was feared and that fear brought respect from everyone who crossed his path along with his attitude towards women and as the story goes there were more than one.

He was known to be stern with the females in his life occasionally he would administer a physical punishment that did not sit right with the father of one of Jesse's women who told Jesse he would kill him if he ever put hands on his daughter again. A couple of weeks later he and this woman got into a disagreement where again Jesse beat her.

Jesse remembered what her father had told him so instead of waiting for her father to find him, Jesse went to him Told him what he had done to his daughter Jesse then pulled a gun and shot him to death.

He served five years in Yuma Penitentiary. As a direct result of that story Johnny made it a point always meet trouble head on regardless of the outcome.

First Life Lesson

Everything was so different in California. The first Christmas was a hot sunny day that had Johnny thinking the end of the world was near since this time of the year all he had ever known was blanketed streets of snow sometimes as much as knee high. Instead everyone was dressed in short pants sandals and tee shirts Not only that but there was a sort of uneasiness within him that made him desperate to return to his home town.

It was the city of Chicago itself that he called Home Not his mother and father or his brothers and sisters, but it was the city, the girls from the public school who protected him from the gangs and took care of him and he needed to go back there to the people in the one place where he felt like somebody The Streets of Chicago. Alone on his way home from school one house away from his the sound of a female voice calls out,

"Hey lil curly head boy come up here and

Talk to me"

He glanced towards the top step of the house next to his and there sat to caramel colored young woman in her Mid 20's dressed in a thin nightgown with a cup of coffee in one hand and a cigarette in the other The flimsy sleeping garment did nothing to conceal that she was not wearing any panties his very first time viewing the anatomy of a woman but he acted as though he didn't see anything as he climbed the steps and sat beside her

"My names Judy what's yours curly head boy? She asked with a warm smile

"Johnny I live next door"

"I know you live next door" she said, "I've seen you before from my window upstairs" It was after 3:00 pm and it was obvious that she was just now waking up for the day

This was the beginning of what would turn out to be his real introduction to an aspect of life that appealed to him and every choice he would make for the greater part of his life. Rules to live by as he would call it Judy had no issues about the profession she chose. She was a "Pro" who worked the streets of Oakland with pride.

In the days and weeks to follow just about every day on his way home from school Judy would be sitting out on the steps where they would talk about everything from politics to the Bible Judy introduced him to her Pimp whom she had bought a red convertible Cadillac Paul and he immediately took a liking to the young man Often times when he would be returning his bottom girl home from a night of working and Johnny was on his way to school Paul would take him

The other students automatically assumed that there was something different about him judging by his being in the company of a known vicious and nefarious Pimp At school he was mostly a loner even though his twin and older brother attend there too still he stayed to himself.

It was during the lunch hour at the high school when three other boys approached him in a manner that caused him to automatically reach into his right pocket for the switch blade he always carried

Suddenly his left arm is pinned behind his back with his right hand being forced in his pocket before he could pull the knife

Two boys held him as another boy William a taller boy who was the leader of the group spoke while the two boys held him when the tall boy hits Johnny in the stomach

Out of nowhere appeared another boy wearing a long black leather coat He spoke sternly to William

"Let him go!" just as the taller boy stops in the middle of delivering another blow

"Come on Marvin this ain't got nothing to do with you"

Marvin takes his hands out of his pockets and speaks slowly

"I said let him go you bigger than he is" as Marvin advanced forward the two boys quickly released Johnny for fear that Marvin was about to attack them then Marvin spoke to Johnny

"Now kick his ass" Johnny turned looked at the taller boy giving him a swift kick to his scrotum bringing him to his knees Students filled the school yard watching the event By the time the teachers arrived they only saw William still on his knees from being kicked in the nuts the other boys had walked away except Marvin who stood with his hands back in his coat pockets

Johnny and Marvin had not met before that day although they had seen one another around the city but Marvin Mc Elroy was feared by most around school known for his boxing skills and too having his way with the ladies

"Say man I owe you one" Johnny expressed to Marvin but with a sly grin he replied

"Man you don't owe me nothing" and walked away with no fan fair or vows to allegiance. It was the way he was on the inside while the world saw something entirely different on the outside. It had been a week before William felt strong enough to face his humiliation at school and at the exact spot where the incident took place by the lunch window William apologized. Roger Gales James Burke Clarence Wells stood at the lunch window when Roger spoke saying,

"Did you guys hear about the summer jobs

With the neighborhood youth core It's on fifty-fifth

And Market"

"Doing what?" Johnny asked

"Cleaning up yards and houses for the elderly in North Oakland" just as his lunch order is passed through the window he accepts He then adds

"And it pays four fifty an hour"

"You can count me in Clarence" confirms

"Me too" James Burkes chimes in

"Yeah you're good long as you live in North Oakland" Roger affirms

This would be a fine opportunity for Johnny to increase his cash flow since he already had two morning newspaper routes that he did every morning on his motorcycle, a Honda 300, but with this extra pay day he would be able to buy himself a car. Already he had his eye on a white convertible olds-mobile so along with the paper routes the second pay check and his side hustle he could have the car in no time.

His side hustle was burglarizing the houses up in the Piedmont hills and his only interest was in the cash no valuables that would be missed just cash. Ultimately his aim was to own a new Cadillac like a real Player and be able to Dress Rest and Request He had no inclination to be a Pimp because in his mind it was nothing but Begging and the truth be known he didn't like the idea of a woman being in his business

His mother knew about his paper route and summer job, but knew nothing about his side hustle His brothers thought other girls were providing him with cash something his twin brother told their mother Providing her with more fuel to curse Johnny

"You just like that damn ole Jesse! You ain't gone be

No good and you goin' straight to hell with your eyes open!"

Little did she realize that the boy found it as a badge of honor to be placed in the same light as his Grandfather Jesse who was his Father's father, a man whom his mother totally despise thus making him a Role Model to her son Although the man had passed away years before Johnny was born his mother talked about him as if it were recent.

He had a plan. As soon as he was able to hustle up a new Cadillac he was going to drive back to Chicago where he knew he would make his fortune and place in the world. As far as what he would do when he got there he had no clue. The only thing on his mind was he had to get back there

Another Lesson

The first of every month was when he would collect from his news –paper routes A time when his mother was well aware and always asked to examine his receipt book so she was able to add up what her cut was after he paid his bill. He had no say in the decision made by a woman who had never worked a day in her life.

His resentment for his mother had taken on a life of its own that day back in 1959, when Johnny was having a severe asthma attack at the Chicago home. The home their father had bought and paid for was actually a huge two story brick home on the west side that actually was composed of four separate apartments each with its own operational kitchen and spacious bedroom.

The boy's bedroom was up the twenty-one winding stair staircase in the middle of the hall. The steam heaters made breathing difficult until he had to go outside dressed in short pants tee shirt and sockless sneakers only then would he be able to breathe easier No one really knew why he would do that and most thought him to be mildly retarded.

On this day in the dead of one of the worst Chicago winters Johnny was having an asthma attack and was trying to make it out of his room and down to long staircase to the front door when suddenly his father rushes through the door the snow and wind blowing violently behind him as he forces the door closed when the boy sees he is now leaning on the closed front door sobbing with tears streaming down his face.

In total shock instantly his breathing difficulty disappeared watching as his Aunt enters the hallway from inside the house meeting his father who cried,

"Look Eva, look what Sue did Had them people

Garnishee my check!" handing a letter to her he was holding in his fist She took it and after a moment she told her brother in law

"Go in there and beat her ass!"

"I can't do that Eva" he sobbed

"I don't see why not" she retorted,

"You go in there and beat her ass

And she won't do that no more".

Johnny had no clue as to what Garnishee meant all he knew was That was his first impression of how treacherous a woman could be and his mother was responsible for bringing the one person in the world he looked up to down to the level of a whimpering pet It was from that day on when the curious youngster started watching his mother to hopefully learn what secret power she held so he would know what to avoid in the future But it was hearing the words out of the mouth of her own sister that stuck in his mind Beat her ass and she won't do that anymore. That was the seed planted in his mind from an early age on the right way to deal with a woman.

Thus formed his opinion about women so as he continued to walk down "The Stroll" past motel after motel an occasional working girl would call out,

"Hey Brown Baby how 'bout letting me

Play Momma tonight I'll take real good care of you" knowing he was still of a very young age but was known to ambush unsuspecting "Tricks" set up by a renegade who didn't feel like flat backing but still had to pay her Pimp. They would have a predesignated place to meet up afterwards and divide the money. His weapon was a 22. Revolver given to him by one of the Ladies

He never made any attempt to make a play for any of the girls instead he was more like their secret enforcer. One night Johnny was exiting the back door of the California Hotel on San Pablo when he observed a man striking a woman violently attempting to drag her into his car The guy was known as a "Gorilla Pimp" like a hungry lion looking for its next meal

Without thinking Johnny yells,

"Hey man let her go!" and began rushing towards the man still holding up the limp body of the woman in his arms stunned from his assault. He lets her go and races for the Drivers side of his sedan de ville She falls to the pavement but grabs hold of Johnny for protection allowing her attacker to get away.

Word of what happened had gotten around the Stroll It seemed to have provided him with an image that earned him a reputation of being one hard and young upcoming street hustler Mostly all of the working girls knew him because of his intervention behind the California Hotel

The red Cadillac pulls to the curb with Paul driving

"Get in Man I got to go down to the Ebony

Hotel and get my money" The Ebony Hotel was located on San Pablo and 34th street in West Oakland next door to Flint's Barbecue one of Oakland's famous landmarks close to downtown. In the car Paul asked

"Man did you know that was Bennie De Bruce

Who was trying to Gorilla Mack a girl who

Belong to another Pimp I know and the Ho

Told her man Big Blue the rest is history"

"What does that mean" Johnny asked and Paul replied

"Man if you respect the Game the Game

Will respect you but if you disrespect it the

Same thing applies only worse" that meant Bennie De Bruce was dead Minutes later Paul does a u-turn on San Pablo to pull in front of the Ebony Hotel where Judy is walking from its entrance to the car. Upon approaching the car Johnny lets the front passenger side window down and Judy squats down,

"Hi Daddy" she says speaking to Paul,

"I see you rollin' with Brown Baby" at the same time passing a thick wad of cash over to Paul as he gives her instructions,

"I got some business out of town so when you

Get through working in the morning I'll come

By for my money" with a departing smile she hurries back to work The Vogue Tires on the Cadillac scream away from the curb.

The moon is full as Paul pilots the sleek machine down the freeway

"Look in the glove box and get that Piece"
The light came on inside the glovebox as Johnny
opened it to see a revolver inside a clip holster
He takes it out closing the box door then slips the
pistol from the holster

A fully loaded 38.

"Keep that 22. For a backup but it's never any

More than three to four guys in the house at

One time nothing you can't handle"

"What's the Lick?"

"A high stake gambling game my attorney put

Me up on in Monterey" A few years before an
angry client wanting Judy for himself attempted
to run Paul down on a street in Palo Alto leaving
him in a coma for three months with permeant
loss and use of his left arm The night it happened
he was with Judy and had to push her out of
the way as the yellow mustang barreled in his
direction but in his cocaine induced state of mind
he stood before the car and swung at it with his
left fist instead of running.

Driving the car with his right arm as he spoke,

"When we get through with this we gonna
drive to

Salinas and western union the money back to us but

I have Judy go pick it up telling her its from my out of

Town Ho. Makes her work harder"

The radio station KSOL with dis jockey Sly Stone playing his new record Everyday People bellowed through the night air creating a feeling of total euphoria. This was the life calling to the young and upcoming hustler Not the aspirations to be anybody's Pimp but to be a man respected and feared by all. There was no place for emotions or being weak.

Surfside Way

———◇———

Beach front property off the shores of the Monterey Peninsula which was a section of homes with only one way in and one way out Paul parked the eye catching vehicle two blocks above after dropping the young armed predator close to the target residence. The sound of the ocean waves crashing against the shore along with the smell the breeze the spray of water with the whipping wind was stimulating

From outside in the dark he could see clearly through the large front picture window Four middle age white men and two blond white women Within seconds he had sized up the project and without any further delay he rang the doorbell. One of the two women arrived to open it without first seeing who it was. But then this sort of thing had not ever happened in the area.

The second the door opened the woman was knocked unconscious by the butt of the 38. Johnny stepped over her to take the other into a strangle hold as he announced his intentions calmly

"Let's not make this a murder so do what I say" holding the woman in a choke hold with one arm while aiming the gun at the four seated men Letting go of the woman he instructed her to go and collect all of the money jewelry and cocaine. Once she had done that Johnny made them all strip down taking off all of their clothes He even made the other woman help undress the unconscious one Tossing their clothes in the blazing fireplace leaving them all naked face down on the cold marble floor as he casually walks away with a large canvas bag back to the car

Back at the car Paul eases out of the area and towards highway 52 for Salinas

"Everything go alright?" Johnny has the canvas bag of loot on the floor between his legs as he goes through it

"Sweet as Bear meat" separating the cash from the wallets the credit cards watches and jewelry listening to KSOL on the radio snorting the cocaine taken in the robbery Steering the Cadillac with his knee Paul takes a snort of the Blow and exclaims

"Ice cream!"

Now in the 11th grade the teenager was learning more from the streets than he would ever in a classroom No it wasn't out of poverty or not having food to eat every day because his father made it a point to provide for his family. But it was out of a need to belong To be accepted and most importantly to be respected. He found all this between Judy Paul and the Streets

Still living at home and maintaining both morning newspaper routes more so to cover for his side hustle he still drove the motorcycle every morning and sometimes during the day. One afternoon he came into the house from riding his bike to discover the back tire needed to be realigned but his twin had the tools last. His brother was on the telephone seated on the sofa when Johnny entered the room asking

"What you do with my tools I need to fix my back tire" while his brother holds up a finger asking him to be quiet while he was on the phone. But

Johnny had a much different idea. He quickly ended his brother's call by quickly pressing the receiver cradle

"My tools I need my tools now!" instead his brother lunges from the sofa wrestling him to the floor. Johnny manages to stay on top planting his fist repeatedly to his face when a knee to the head sends Johnny sailing off of his brother. His father walked in to see the two boys fighting and with his right knee kneed the aggressive son in his head. Before Johnny realized it was his father he shouts,

"Muthafucka what you kick me for!" and it was too late to take it back

"Boy what you say" in a slow low tone of voice

"I think we need to step in the back yard"

"You damn right lets go!" Too late to back down now the whole family of sisters and brothers all filled into the back yard to witness their father deliver a beating to their brother. None of his brothers ever dared to stand up against him or challenge his authority.

His mind was running a thousand miles per second What had he gotten himself into But there was no turning back as he walked quickly to the middle of the large back yard with fist clinched and turned squaring off to battle with his father who saunters towards the angry boy and he didn't see it coming when his father delivered a blurred speed strike to his chest knocking him backwards. He throws a right hand Johnny sees stars from the blow staggering backwards but stays on his feet All the while his mother and siblings are cheering their father on to punish him as though they were sitting ring side at a prize fight.

Another shot like that and its good night Irene Johnny thought then he remembered his father recently underwent a hernia operation and Johnny ducked a right hand and caught his father with a smashing left hook directly on the healing wound causing him to drop to the ground on one knee in pain All cheering ceased but turned into screams of shock as Johnny just turned and walked down the driveway and did not return home for three days.

Everything was happening so fast. The last thing in the world he would ever think of was raising his hands to his father. But he did and there was no taking it back. Noticing the black ford pickup his father drove parked outside in front of the house Johnny entered the front door to the eerily silent house. He closes the front door and walks the hallway to the living room door. He opened it. The room was dark with the exception of the light coming from the television screen that his father sat in front of watching the evening news

Johnny enters the room as his father continues to focus his eyes on the TV screen not once looking away from it

"Come on in Son Have a seat" indicating the empty sofa chair next to his recliner There is no sound on the black and white TV only images of a news anchor man sitting behind a desk reporting the news

"You eat yet?" his father asked in a slow relaxed tone of voice

"Yeah" the boy replied respectfully and his father spoke calm and slowly

"Good Now listen. You're a man now so the next

Time we have a disagreement I'm a get my gun

And shoot you"

"I understand" Johnny said then his father commanded

"Now gone upstairs and take a bath you been out

In them streets doing who knows what" Without comment the cautious young man gets up and leaves the room. He was cautious of how his father was going to take being brought to his knees in front of the whole family. He was a proud man and by all rights he should be, but the fear he once had for his father is all gone The only thing he has left is respect for the man who gave him life

One week later Johnny was caught out of bounds on a closed campus school. He would leave campus during the lunch hour on his motorcycle and case unoccupied homes in the affluent parts of Oakland. Little did he know that the school had changed its policies about leaving campus during school hours lunch time included Johnny missed the memo and

Had gotten locked out which ultimately landed him in the Vice Principals office an entirely different man than the one from Berkeley High This guy acted as if he was always angry with life and Johnny knew what to expect once he got to his office now seated in front of his brown oak desk

"You people seem to think you can do what

You want" getting up from his seat behind the desk to walk around and stand over Johnny pointing his finger disrespectfully in Johnny's face but when he accidently spits in the boy's face while scolding him Johnny leaped to his feet right fist clinched and caught the left side of his jaw knocking him to the floor Johnny only turned and walked out of the office knowing that this was real trouble so his school days were over.

Not only that but so was his home life There would be none after this remembering what his father told him and this clearly would create the next disagreement.

The Choice

———◇———

Johnny rented a motel with kitchen and weekly rates near the park on Broadway It was small. Not quite what he had been use to but at least it was his and he had no one to answer to. Now at the age of seven-teen going on eight-teen life was about to take on a whole new meaning. He decided the newspaper routes were history The money was too slow although getting up early in the morning before the sun was always the best part of his day

Everything was different now He was different With his end from the lick in Monterey he was able to pay his rent up for six months The place was furnished so all he needed to do was buy food. He learned how to cook from watching his father who was a chef by profession Really it was about the only positive thing he could say that he did learn from him

Since his father had to co-sign for the motorcycle he left it and bought the convertible olds-mobile from the Monterey take He was walking to the parking lot there at the motel when this all of four foot five sexy dark skin mini skirt wearing woman steps out of a black Mustang with a green convertible top and says to him

"Excuse me sir but do you stay here?" she asks Johnny who replies

"Excuse me Bitch but are you the poleece?"

Immediately she recognizes her mistake

"Oh! Excuse you See I live here and you been

Parking where I park for the last three days"

Johnny looks at her in almost disbelief

"What!" But before he allows his true nature to assault her for being so bold to challenge him he replies

"Oh I see had I been aware of you and known

There was a fee due then I would of known

Exactly who to go to So now that I do I'm Johnny what's your name"

Clearly this was an introduction more so an invitation and the young predator was still in training. Even though his mind was not on being or trying to be anything like Paul his aim only was to establish a cash flow This little Black Spasm was clearly making her presence known and all that was good but not for free.

"Fae My Name is Fae" as she stands all of less than five feet tall and Johnny towering above her says

"Okay I'll tell you what Fae this is what we're

Going to do I like you and you like me so we're

Not going to waste time Life's too short for that"

Without another word being spoken between them she goes into her bra to produces a thick wad of money and hands it to Johnny He then says to her

"Now you can park on any side of me you want to

My room is 201 upstairs I'll be back in an hour"

Truth is Johnny had no idea of what to do next The only thing he remembered was what Judy had taught him. Leaving the Motel he drove over to the barber shop Paul's father owned on Grove street in north Oakland to share the news of his first Cop with Paul along with instructions on what to do next

The Barber shop was actually a front for exclusive gambling games where high rollers like the Ward brothers Ted and Frank Entertainers like the Whispers. Kenny Gales and his brother Roger would show up driving Roger's 1932 Cord while Kenny would dazzle the audience with his vocal stylings

Upstairs above the Barber Shop was an apartment Behind it down stairs was where the gambling games took place but the apartment is where Paul junior would hold meetings as well as entertain new prospects Two of his girls Panama and Darleen are sitting on the sofa while Paul is seated at the table with James Burkes snorting blow when Johnny walks in counting cash in his hands

"What you do hit another lick" Paul asks Johnny

"Nope choosing fee from a hooker at the same spot

Where I got a room"

It came to a total of two hundred in twenties placing it back into his pocket

"I had been seeing her around there but I wasn't

Gonna crack on her cause I like mine light bright and

Damn near white" Paul intervenes

"Man just like to a Trick pussy ain't got no color

To a hustler the only color that matters is Green" raising the coke spoon to his nose

"Oh don't get me wrong I'm not turning down nothing but my collar" he invites Johnny

"Have a hit a this before you go school your

New game It'll have you just right" Johnny obliges taking one in each nostril then heads for the door

Back at the motel in the room at the other end of the hall on the first floor Johnny is in Fae's room One with a kitchen just like his Seated at the table he asks,

"So tell me what you do" and she replies

"Rather than flip Tricks I get more money hitting licks"

"Oh! The girl got nerve I like that" Thinking to himself this would be a perfect business arrangement Johnny had found his "Bonnie"

She moved about the room and goes under the bed to produce a sawed off single barrel shotgun and presents it to him

"Yes we got work to do!" he says with glee as he is checking out the blue steel weapon as she reports,

"Sometimes me and my girlfriend go on licks

Together but I haven't see her in a few weeks"

"What you think she's busted?" he ask

"No it's probably that worthless guy she's got".

As the days progressed into weeks Johnny met her friend Phyllis who was more to his liking Light Bright and damn near white She told Fae that she had finally had enough of the guy she was with and together they shared her apartment she became part of the crew Although the thought was on his mind he not once made an advance towards her If it was going to be anything she would have to make the first move

For the next two years the trio would travel out of the Bay Area to near- by towns to execute robberies of jewelry stores even as far as Portland Oregon after Fae and Phillis had learned from other girls who worked the streets in Washington state and Portland where the security on the high end stores was a real joke

After one week on the road Johnny and his ladies leased a three bedroom home in North Oakland with two car garage and back yard

Life was good

Two years went by in a blur He had given the olds mobile to Fae and Phillis buying himself a 68 triple black convertible Coupe De Ville and a 1955 Chevy hot rod that he drove on the weekends or for fun. The Hog was to announce his ability to clock a dollar Johnny had not seen his parents or any of his siblings in going on three years until one night he was coming out of Hy's restaurant and bar on Telegraph and Mc Author when he hears someone calling his name He turns to see its his twin and older brother home on leave from the Navy

It was early evening just as Johnny stepped out onto the sidewalk when his two brothers were truly glad to see him But in his cocaine induced state of mind he was in no mood to play and pulled a 38. Ordering

"I said back up!" causing them to freeze in their tracks as he walks out to the curb gets in his car and speeds away It wasn't that he meant to be hostile or mean truth is he didn't relate to them as being his family as a result of their past history But they were grown now and they never played games when they were younger so too late to start now

Reality Check

The idea to take off the White Front United Grocer's Wear House in Fremont was where migrant workers would go to cash their paychecks this meant the job would be in and out with ease. The plan was Johnny enters announces the play one girl goes to the safe the other to the registers

There is one clerk behind the counter and three men face down on the floor with their hands behind their heads. Standing between the door watching the clerk on the floor inside the office and the three out in the front it only took that second for the clerk to hit the alarm The police station was less than a mile way

The two girls exit first with the money heading back to the car Moments later Johnny emerges from the building securing the two pistols under his suit vest as he yells ahead to the girls

"Run go on get to the car!" Suddenly the sound of tires screaming next to him in the street

"Hold it Union city Police Officer!" Immediately Johnny pulls both guns and fires at the police car causing both officers to duck for cover giving Johnny enough time to run in the opposite direction. Within seconds the entire area is swarming with police cars even highway patrol at the call of Shot's being fired

Funny how nervousness can trigger a form of hysteria even though bullets are flying and the thought of death is near still you laugh knowing full and well that this is no joke just as the force from one of the bullets strikes him in his neck causing him to fall face first to the ground but still conscious crawling on his hands and knees until he his swarmed by blue uniforms kicking him in the head with steel toed boots until he is no longer moving.

Taken to the jail ward at the county hospital where he was x-rayed to locate the bullet in the lower left side of his neck but the doctors said no it was logged between his fourth and fifth vertebrae too close to vital nerves while he remained in a coma from the vicious kicks For the next thirteen days he would remain in a comatose state

Fae and Phillis were almost caught that day not wanting to leave Johnny but reluctantly Fae drove cautiously away with Phillis down in the back seat to avoid detection from the heavy police presence.

Making it back to the house both women were close to panic until Fae broke the silence

"The best thing we can do is sit still and wait"

"Did you hear all those gun shots? "Phillis asked nervously

"What if he's hurt" Phillis rushes to turn on the local news to see if there was any report

A news helicopter appeared after the gun fire but filmed Johnny being kicked in the head face down covering his face Both girls scream in horror they knew that neither could run the risk of going to the hospital but that was just a chance they would have to take According to the news report he was taken to the county hospital After totally altering their appearance it was a race to the County

Thirteen days after the Robbery Fae is in the hospital room arranging a vase of flowers by the sun in the window He stirs in bed moving with a groan of pain in his head Looking across the room he can see a woman arranging flowers in a vase but he does not know who she is Amnesia had him where he did not even know what his own name was and felt

Too embarrassed to ask instead he spoke asking

"What happened" as she walked closer to the bed to secure the blanket over him,

"You're alright now You been out for a while

How do you feel?" she asked cautiously caressing his face he answered

"My neck is stiff My head is throbbing and I ache all over" he notices the hospital visitor's pass attached to her jacket Her name FAE but still no memory of her or who she is In addition there was a plain clothed white man sitting in a chair by the door A police officer assigned to watch the hospitalized prisoner just as Judy walks in presenting her pass and identification to the man then goes to his bed side

With a warm bright smile she embraces him Tears well up in her eyes

"Man! You had me scared out of my mind" He looked closely at her tear stained face but could not remember who she was

All he knew was that he had this impending feeling of embarrassment at not being able to remember anything and had no idea about what to do. This all has to be a dream he thought. That's it! It's all a dream and soon he would wake up Fae stood by silently as Judy talked with him

"Man what was you thinking about?" He replied with uncertainty

"I don't know I mean I can't remember nothing" Judy then said

"When I came in I told the front desk that

I was your aunt I spoke with your doctor

And he told me this might happen but he

Couldn't tell me how long it would last"

"So now what?" Johnny asked and she answered

"You know you got a case but me and Paul got you with a lawyer"

"What kind of case?" He asks

"You really don't remember do you Man they had you

All on TV"

All the while she spoke he was searching his thoughts trying to absorb what she was claiming he had done. But nothing It was like a black void a blank screen in his head that revealed nothing….

FAST FORWARD
1973

The Fremont Robbery earned Johnny a ten year to life Sentence in Soledad State Prison. While in prison he taught himself how to use a typewriter since he felt the only way he would be able to communicate with the outside world was to be able to express himself through words but his penmanship was not all that great.

Every day he would spend hours in his cell reading the dictionary to improve his vocabulary and develop a form of communication with the outside world while every morning he had to attend classes in the education area because he did not have a high school diploma but his only concern was the room where the typewriters were kept but the math and other classes he would skip.

As a result of not following the rules in prison and attending all of his classes he was often placed on C.T.Q. (Confined to quarters) during the weekends but during the week every day he could be found out in the gravel pit filled with free weights flat benches incline benches decline benches dip and pull up bars everything to cultivate a prize winning physique

Soledad State prison in the 70's was known for its violence and killings behind the prison walls while its visiting policies made it easy for the convicts to reach out to emotionally deprived women looking for that mister Right to come and sweep her off her feet the only difference was she had to come to him

I suppose it was something about "Bad Boys" women found exciting to be associated with especially the ones who were always told to stay away from those type of guys Paula Benson was no exception. She had a cousin serving time in Soledad for armed robbery who was the first prisoner to be able to get married in the California prison system

It was at that ceremony where Johnny met who would turn out to be his first wife As far as he was concerned she had no appeal what so ever and he made no serious attempt to pursue her while she made it clear that no matter what she wanted him to be with her when he got out

Johnny learned early in life that the best game in the world is the Truth. He made it a point that she knew about the three other girls who would visit him from time to time Paula even showed up one weekend when Johnny was visiting with Phyllis and he invited her to sit with them but she declined and chose to sit alone. Johnny had asked them all to let him know in advance when they were coming, but that time she chose not to. If this was her attempt to establish her position in his life it failed

Another time she showed up in the middle of the week but rode the greyhound bus from Los Angeles instead of driving her car The problem was that visitors who arrive by greyhound must leave by 2:00 to get the bus back to LA The visiting room guard announced

"Any visitor who rode the greyhound bus must

Leave the visiting room in order to catch the

Next bus back to Los Angeles, the next one

Isn't until 6:00 pm except for those staying

For a family visit" Immediately Paula said to Johnny

"Oh! Get us one of those"

"What!" he shot back "No we can't do that so

Go on and I'll write you tonight"

A family Visit required the participants to be legally married and in no way a consideration when it came to Paula There was absolutely not one thing he found remotely attractive about her other than her being a supervisor at the post office with good credit But even that when it came to her his saying was "All money ain't good money"

From the moment she left the visiting room she was plotting her next move to reel in the handsome muscular and eloquent young man She had no children was four years older than Johnny and was going to do whatever she had to do in order to get this fine specimen of a man

The following weekend Paula arrived at the prison to visit and once inside while sitting at a table with Johnny the catholic priest enters the visiting room like he does every weekend except this time he is walking directly to Johnny who out of respect stand up extending his hand to the priest

"Good afternoon father"

"John" he smiles then says "And this must be Paula"

Johnny has no idea what is going on but invites the father to have a seat there at the table and as he obliges he says'

"I guess the only thing left is to set the date" causing Johnny to ask

"Date for what?" is when Paula speaks up stating

"See, I wrote the father a letter and told him that

You had got me pregnant before you came to

Prison but I had a miscarriage" Johnny sat listening and could not believe what he was hearing as she continued with her confession

"By me losing the baby I figure that was

God telling me to do it the right way so

I wrote the father asking him to marry us"

"So- the priest exhales in asking what the date will be Johnny says to Paula,

"Make it light on yourself and tell him what

Date you want" Unbeknown to the priest or Paula Johnny is annoyed to the point where as soon as the priest exits the visiting room he tells Paula that she too has to leave clearly restraining himself from saying what he really wanted to say and curse her severely for what he looked at as she was playing him something he was not going to allow which meant he would be taking Paula off of his visiting listOnce back inside the prison there were these two other convicts who Johnny associated with George Wiley and Donnie Henderson aka "Skippy" both being three and four years older George was in the forgery and fraud business while Donnie was a heroin dealer on a possession beef.

George was considered the Player out of the trio as well as having come from a considerably comfortable home life being raised as an only child by a white mother and a black father who put him through college, but George chose a much different route than that of his Engineering dad

The three were seated at a table for the evening meal as Johnny speaks to George

"Man I'm not jumping the broom with that Dog

In fact I'm taking that bitch off my visiting list" causing Skippy to laugh

"I'm serious" Johnny injects but Skippy then says

"Think about it Man you'll be able to

Go on family visits" but Johnny replies

"Man please I wouldn't be able to get it up"

"Awe come on man she can't be that bad

And besides pussy ain't got no face"

"That may apply to a Trick but

I don't think with my dick" Johnny states flatly just when George asks him

"Didn't you go to the parole board last march?"

"Yeah I seen them clowns"

"What they say?"

"I told you back then that they downed me

Another year said I didn't have any responsibilities"

"And there it is!" George exclaimed with enthusiasm

"Your automatic responsibility and the next time you

Go to the Board they can't use that as a reason to

Deny you parole twice they got to come up with

Something else but if you don't give um nothing no incident reports

They got to give you a release date" Suddenly it made sense especially since he held no belief in the sacrament of marriage He would be getting the better end of the deal

The following week when he requested her to be there for the weekend carefully he explained at the table

"Now listen I can't promise you anything because

I don't know what I'm going to do when I get

Out of here- cutting him off she pleads

"I don't care what you do as long as you're

With me" Little did she realize that it was the letters he writes her that she is in love with not him as a person who she had no clue

She informed the priest that the following month of March was when they would take the vows which meant nothing at all to him. There were mental scars in his mind that can never erased from the years he spent watching his mother plot against his father when all he did was to do the best he could to keep her happy No especially not with this one.

Realizing that he now had a serious game plan on being able to get a parole date at his next hearing Johnny made it a point to attend all of his classes so not to give them any reason to deny him a release His attendance improved while the only class he excelled in was Typing because that was what he knew would be to his benefit for years to come

Now that he had married Paula there in prison they could have a family visit which was scheduled for that following weekend. Johnny gave her specific instructions on what to bring and how to bring it The only thing on his mind was being able to mentally escape prison for two days out in a mobile home trailer.

He told her to buy a plastic flask and fill it with Brandy then conceal it somewhere on her body the same thing with the weed put it in plastic so not to set off the metal detectors. The trailer already contained pots and pans to cook with She brought a homemade carrot cake Sirloin steaks fruit and bottled beverages

One of the rules was that he had to stand outside the trailer three times a day to be counted by the guard in the gun tower but other than that there was no supervision That first night Paula prepared a meal of sirloin steak cheese broccoli rice gravy with mixed vegetable salad

While Paula cooked Jonny smoked and drank fulfilling his opportunity to feel free for just a little while. As far as intimacy with his now wife it was the farthest thing on his mind

The alcohol combined with the smoke had him in a total state of euphoria Peace that is difficult to find behind the prison walls except when you learn how to redirect your thoughts and feelings and accept the fact that this is only a temporary condition

Wearing only his prison boxers smoking on the sofa Paula came and sat beside him unable to keep her hands off his well sculpted physique All the while he is thinking about how he will get out of not having any intentions or desire to be intimate with her so he made up the excuse of having to check in three times a day was distracting but when the last count was over he would feel differently or at least he would make her think so

By the time the last count was over he had gotten so high until all she could do was to attempt oral sex on him but even that did not work and he would go straight to sleep The next night the same thing until it was time for the visit to be over

Once back inside he continued to participate in programs that would earn him more privileges and an early board appearance granting him a

July 13 1973 release date.

At that time Paula lived in a one bedroom apartment on Tamarind in Compton but after being in in tiny cell for the last four years Johnny told her that he needed some space and did not care to live in a small apartment

Through her credit union at the post office she purchased a two bed-room home with separate garage spacious back yard with ten different fruit trees and in the garage she had bought him a black on black in black 1965 Thunderbird along with a complete wardrobe of clothes

It was on this day when his first born was conceived A baby boy while it wouldn't be until she was showing some five months later that he even believed that she was pregnant because the truth was he was so high he did not remember being intimate with her

Twenty-Four years old and a father with a new born son by a mother who meant absolutely nothing to Johnny but now there is a child who is clearly his seed The morning he was born Johnny just barely made it in time from the airport to the hospital After being given a gown and face mask he was allowed to enter the delivery where in a half intoxicated state Johnny blurted out upon first seeing his son

"Look at the nuts on that boy" meaning to say "It's a Boy" but that was how he heard it in his head and that was how it came out causing the nurses and doctor to blush in embarrassment while patting Paula on the head where she still lay on the delivery table saying

"You did good Thanks for that"

Right then and there he made his choice to stay for the sake of his son his first born which had nothing to do with his mother something that she did not understand In truth over the following months she would act oddly when it came to Johnny spending time with his son excluding her She was possessive to a fault.

Once when his new born was old enough to sit up on his own Johnny would place a large pillow on the console of the black thunderbird and with his right arm around the infant he would drive about Los Angeles during the day before he had to work the night shift at Lockheed in Downey

Without thinking twice one hot summer afternoon Johnny decides to take his son with him to go park by the ocean in San Pedro up by Point Fermin a grassy park atop rugged costal bluffs featuring a playground amphitheater trails and picnic areas. Sitting parked smoking a joint in the car with his son seated on the console beside him looking out across the water down below

By the time he drove back home to Compton Paula was running around in a panic in the front yard as he pulled into the driveway she rushes to the passenger side of the car opens it and quickly snatched the baby from the car all the while screaming clutching the boy close to her

"Don't you ever take my child away from here to

Be around them Ho's you be messing with!" while she is rushing into the house with child in arms Johnny walks into the house just as she is placing the child in his crib and as she stands to confront Johnny he viciously slaps her in the face knocking her to the floor but she makes a futile attempt to strike him in retaliation only to be met with a single punch that sent her crashing into the glass coffee table on her back kicking and screaming until he grabs her by the throat to silence her

Slowly she begins to struggle less and less until her arms drop limp to her side and he roughly tosses her on to the sofa where she begins to cough and recompose herself as the infuriated man who was seething with anger

"Bitch That is my son and don't you think you

Can tell me what I can and can't do Now get your

Ass up and clean this shit up" Needless to say that did not ever happen again Still she craved the attention he only displayed with the child that she carried for nine months and gave birth to so was it so hard for him to feel a portion of that same love for her

For at least a week or two after having pushed his violent button Paula would be meek and submissive as long as Johnny was around and not out in the streets with the prostitutes she knew he associated with one in particular lived only three blocks away which he kept no secret He has always believed that the best game in the world is the truth, while at the same time he would not allow his girl Gail to disrespect Paula by showing up at their door for any reason She knew to send a messenger one of his neighbors

It was the summer in the mid 70's having had to walk away from his job at Lockheed Johnny was seated on the floor in the bedroom while Paula was rolling his hair in rollers from the Perm she had just finished giving him when the sound of a car horn blowing in front of the house Paula gets up and goes to investigate only Moments pass before she returns saying calmly,

"I think you better go answer that" reclaiming her seat on the side of the bed Johnny gets to his feet and goes to the front door. It's Gail

"Bitch what did I tell you!" She is clearly under the influence of Red Devils alcohol and who knows what else

"I need to talk to you Johnny" slurring speech struggling to open the latch on the front cyclone fence gate as he stands at the screen door speaking to her

"I said go home and I'll be around there in a minute" but she still attempts to open the gate Johnny walks towards her just as she opens it and takes one step inside Immediately he grabs a hand full of her

Long thick red hair and drags her back to the car doubled parked in front of his house with the motor still running. There was a female passenger Gail had in the car with her but at the sight of Johnny dragging her by her hair She is so loaded that she can barely walk let alone drive But Johnny forces her back into the car places her right foot on the accelerator then slamming the gear shift into drive with tires screaming and the smell of rubber burning on the asphalt the large sedan slams into a parked car a few feet down the street.

From that point on it seemed to be one problem after another On State parole he found himself facing a parole violation for being in possession of a fire arm and associating with a known prostitute. While sleeping one afternoon laying on top of the made bed with his infant son beside him asleep The weed he had smoked was good and the Boone's Farm Apple wine was cold. The whole bottle

The next thing he knew Paula was shaking him awake telling him that his parole officer was there to see him She was holding his son and he never felt her take him from the bed. He was out like a light bulb until

His head began to clear as he sat up on the side of the bed. The parole officer was already standing over him as he sat up trying to make out what he was saying and why was he there but when he watched the man reaching for his handcuffs Johnny shoved him into the wall as he leaped on to the bed about to make his exit when he saw the two blue Compton police uniforms standing out in the hall

"What the fuck is goin' on!" standing in the middle of the king size bed

"I got a report of you shooting at some women

Gail was her name" the PO stated

"A Ho! Are you serious You taking the word of

A Ho!" snatching up a pillow there on the bed throwing it at the agent not realizing there is a 38. Revolver beneath it One of the officers out in the hall see's it and shouts

"Gun!" Having forgotten he always slept with it there he quickly picked it up with two fingers and handed it to the officer as he stepped in with

His gun drawn about to shoot saying,

"This ain't mine It's hers" not that it would do any good since that was his main parole restrictions NO Guns and the P.O. announces

"I got to take you in now Johnny" and without further resistance he walked out to the police car with the officers and was driven to the old County, Jail in down town Los Angeles to await the next parole hearing that would determine how much more time he would have to serve for the violation of being in possession of a loaded firearm

Major Harris was singing over the loud speakers throughout the barred facility Love Won't Let Me Wait creating a kind of serenity in the middle of all the madness slamming steel doors constant yelling or crying until late at night when the moon is full and the whole floor is silent while the soft melodic sounds envelope the air

For three months that was the only peace he looked forward to every night when the cell block was quiet He was being housed in a four man cell with three other parole violators when his cell door opens and his name is directed to step out of the cell with all belongings as a result of being reinstated back on parole Without taking anything with him he spoke to his soon to be former cell mates half way out

"You guys can have everything I'm gone!" and took off running down the cell block to be released all the while wondering was this some kind of mistake and there would be a prison bus waiting to take him back

But instead Paula was waiting for him out in the parking lot to take him home He walked swiftly to the orange beetle with the white stripe across the trunk and got in asking

"What happened?"

"You had a parole hearing this morning and

I asked to be there I told them the gun was

Registered to me and showed them my papers

Proving I bought it before you got out

They told me if I got rid of it they would not

Violate you"

"Then hurry up and get me out of here before

Something else happens"

Trying Times

One's true nature manages to always manifest itself no matter how hard you try to be different After being released from LA County remaining in Los Angeles was getting to be not very welcoming and it was clearly time to Break Camp He had stop reporting for parole and relocated back to the San Francisco Bay area with Gail

Living in the Fillmore district where life out on the streets was like life in the wildest jungles of Africa Once the sun had faded from the sky if you were not seasoned with what is going on around you surely no doubt you will end up as a victim a Trick or dead

Gail was no stranger to the corner of Fillmore and Eddy where the Ladies of The Night gathered dressed in their finest and call out to the

Passing cars with only one man in it

"Hey daddy lets have some fun" While another one chants

"Ten an two baby what you wanna do

Two dollars for the room a ten for

Whatever you want me to do"

It was like a Circus but with a different type of
Clown some were women out selling their bodies
while others were selling drugs to the users
who sit out openly with needles of heroin being
injected into their arms causing some to go limp
slobber at the mouth and nod off into another
world where nothing matters

Johnny was walking out of the Walgreen's on
Height and Fillmore when he notices the white
Rolls Royce. Its Kenny Gales parking in front of
the Blues Bar on Height near the corner He walks
the short distance across the street

"Ken Ekool what's happening man" Johnny
speaks jovially

"Good thing I know you an entertainer
otherwise

I would a thought you was doing some serious

Hustling out here" the two "Mack Slap" hands

"Shee-it I am hustling I'm booked to preform
here tonight If you around you ought to stop by the

Show starts at ten"

"That'll work in fact I've got some music I
wrote

I'd like you to look at"

"For sure just come on through" and Johnny walks away back to his car

From the corner of Height street he drives straight up Fillmore towards Eddy just as he approaches the corner he can see Gail and a very large man rushing up behind her with what looks like a butcher knife and with his left hand he grabs her by the hair and with his right hand he decapitates her holding her severed head in his left hand

From behind the man are flashing lights red white blue then the sound of multiple guns being fired until he falls to the ground dead still holding the severed head in his hand Johnny looks on in disbelief frozen in awe at what he just witnessed Everything happened so fast until it was like a blur The street became more and more condensed with police cars and news helicopters flying over the scene.

Johnny left his car in the middle of the street as he walked closer to where the headless body of his girl lay sprawled in a pool of still gushing blood. The police were putting up yellow crime scene tape preventing people from contaminating the evidence Her body lay only a few feet away until it is covered with a sheet by one of the uniformed officers

Other working girls crowd around clearly in shock. One girl looks at Johnny recognizing him as the one who Gail told her was her man after he had dropped her off on the corner of Fillmore and Eddy She goes to his side

"Johnny? I'm Gwen I knew your girl we was working together tonight She told me she had a date an asked me to hold her trap money we do that looking out for each other"

Totally emotionless Johnny takes in what just happened realizing that he has to rely on his back up plan now that his main girl was gone Truth be known it was what he preferred over waiting on a woman to sustain his financial needs The barrel of a gun always worked faster than any other thing he knew.

His first thought was to get in touch with Paul but he remembered Paul was in the hospital from being poisoned by one of his disgruntled ladies with Fentanyl but it didn't kill him but paralyzed him from the neck down leaving him with only partial use of his one good arm

Phyllis and Fae were still with him which meant that once again he was in need of the assistance of a woman Fae was the only one between the two girls who had three regulars while Phyllis had none and did not work the stroll She was not of a mind to go that route because she was versed in dealing drugs weed and pills Whatever they chose to do to in order to hold up their end was their choice because Johnny made it clear that he was nobody's pimp

Unlike Paul who would preach that he had big broad shoulders pretty brown eyes waves for the babes and curls for the girls inviting them to put the money on his dresser claiming to break a brick choke a stick and drown in a drip of water for his pimping Johnny's cliché' was that he simply was in the Life to get paid and game was meant to be sold not told keeping what he was really doing between himself Fae and Phyllis

His ultimate ambition was to make that one big score where he would be able to sit back for the rest of his life. But most importantly he had to be the one to put it all together alleviating a claim any woman could stake on his prosperity which was nothing more than an emotional blemish left from the mental scars inflicted by his mother

Johnny had a friend Donald Rae Randolph a seemingly mild mannered guy around the same age as Johnny but was virtually born into the Game His mother ran a brothel and speakeasy from the time he was born The only baby sitters he ever knew were Ladies of the night and each one considered the young Donald Rae as their own guiding him through life as he grew.

Donald Rae had always been the one to go to when putting together a fat Lick and if he didn't have one he knew where to go The two met at the Quarter Pound hamburger stand on sixty-fifth and east fourteenth in Oakland Donald Rae in his White Customized Cadillac pulls in and he gets out Johnny is standing at the order window outside

"What's going on with you man long time no see" Speaks Donald Rae with his right hand extended the two shake hands warmly

"Man I'm just trying to keep my head above water

Know of a Play with a big pay day?"

"As a matter of fact" Donald Rae says with a bright smile "funny you

Should ask" his way of letting him know that in deed he did One of his girls had a client who was trying to unload some Bearer Bonds worth over one million and he had another girl at a bank who whole cash them His take was twenty percent.

The Mark with the Bonds unbeknown to Johnny was a federal agent who had a habit of being with call girls seriously "Under Cover" against company policy even criminally Should it ever be discovered the agent could risk possible jail time not to mention his removing evidence from a federal property for the purpose of selling to the highest bidder would earn him an additional twenty-five years in a federal penitentiary

White forty five years old clean cut having been an agent for the last seven years Married with two children but insanely infatuated with one of the girls in Donald Rae's stable They only meet at the Biltmore in San Francisco for their appointments sometimes lasting an entire weekend with her price one thousand dollars per night opposed to the Fillmore district He made it a point to always provide the best for her even though her price was a grand per night Donald Rae would say

"I don't just deal with the ass I deal with class"

Dressed in a three pieces handmade Jack Williams suit Johnny walks into the lavish hotel heading towards the lounge and bar area The girl Desiree always met the client there where they would have drinks maybe visit one of the saunas or large Olympic size swimming pool sort of like a form of Foreplay especially since he enjoyed the looks and stares he would get from both men and women seeing him with the long hair brunet sexy Mulatto

The plan was that she would slip a knock out drug in his drink once she knew exactly where the bonds were in turn she would tell Johnny who would retrieve them Everything had gone according to plan The Agent told her via pillow talk that the bonds were locked in the trunk of his unmarked car out in the parking lot One drink was all it took and he was out like a light

With keys in hand Johnny simply walked the parking lot partially obscuring his face pressing the automatic door lock and horn until he found the car opened the trunk removed the two brief cases and walked away in the night The next day it was front page news FEDERAL AGENT FOUND SHOT TO DEATH WITH PROSTITUTE AT BILTMORE HOTEL the security cameras show Johnny entering the hotel. Parking lot security cameras show him going into the trunk of the agent's car and removing two bags thus making him suspect number one. The only clear view of his face is from the hotel lobby while only his clothing was compared to the second but clearly it was Johnny

Now at the house in Oakland with Fae and Phyllis Fae runs in the house with the morning San Francisco Chronical in her hand

Johnny had delivered the bonds to Donald Rae that same night before making his way in He slept alone in the master bedroom of the home when Fae came charging in with the paper

to find him standing in front of a full length mirror getting dressed Handing the paper to him without saying a word he looks at himself in the paper then reads about the agent being killed

Within that same space of time came a pounding at the front door It was the F.B.I. Opening the door to face an ocean of guns pointed in his direction backed with a search warrant they find half a gram of coke some weed guns 38. Along with a 357 and take Johnny handcuffed to 450 Bryant Street to the Federal Building and lock up where he is charged with the murder of the agent.

The federal holding facility was on the very top floor above the court rooms on Golden Gate Ave. but the prisoners are being held clear across the Bay in the North County Jail in Oakland while awaiting trial located on 7th street across from Mexicali Rose Mexican Restaurant.

All federal prisoners are housed on the 5th floor separated from the prisoners with State charges then bused to the federal court house across the Bay. Johnny was sent straight to the hole.

Racking his brain trying to figure out how this could have happened. There was no way Donald Rae had anything to do with it since he had been with Desiree since childhood and he was not that type to kill indiscriminately. No there was something going on that was about to send him to the Electric chair unless he could prove he didn't do it which might be difficult to do locked up.

The circumstantial evidence was more than enough to get a warrant to charge him with federal offences Burglary of federal property by going in the agents car and capital murder of a federal agent with special circumstances by it being premeditated.

Further investigation of the hotel security footage in the hallway leading to the room where the body was found at no time was there footage of Johnny anywhere near that hallway only the maids with their cleaning carts along with other residents going in and out of rooms

One frame shows the agent with Desiree stepping out of the room together while the maid enters to clean. Another frame shows the two returning. A different frame shows another maid entering the room with a stack of towels in her arms. Another frame shows her leaving. Another frame shows a maid entering the room to find the two dead bodies.

Further investigation would lead the F.B.I. to the wife who had found out about the affair through home bank records. She planned on collecting a large sum of money from his being killed in the line of duty along with his pension "Hell has no fury like a woman scorned"

Still there was the matter of the car burglary of a federal vehicle plus the guns and drugs discovered during the search of his home which earned him a fifteen year sentence in federal prison

Unlike the State system the federal prison system had more programs geared towards rehabilitation than the State and Johnny took the opportunity to learn everything about home building He found that he liked working with his hands actually seeing what he created.

TIME PASSED
1990's

His son would be around fifteen or sixteen years old by now although Johnny had not seen the boy since he was three. Early one morning on the Harbor freeway Johnny is driving from San Diego with both Fae and Phillis when he spots the orange super beetle with a wide white stripe across the hood It was Paula on her way to work. Traffic is at a virtual standstill making it easy for her to pull along his passenger side and look inside the car as she yelled

"Hey! Are you coming by to see your son?" all the while she is straining to see who the women are He shouts back through the open window

"Yeah I'll be through there" As traffic begins to pick up she asks

"What time?" but without a response he presses the power window button and raises the window without answering driving away until The flow and speed of traffic increases and he speeds away down the freeway.

From his rear view mirror he can see that she is attempting to follow him but he maneuvers off the freeway before she can change lanes. Later that afternoon he drives to Compton and knocks on the door Paula opens it wearing a robe clutching it together. Johnny steps inside asking

"Where's the boy"

"Oh he outside playing but I want to talk to

You first- Johnny is not having that and cuts her off

"No you call the boy right now or I'm leaving!" as he turns walking back out the front door with Paula trailing behind him she first looks inside his car to see it is empty then she yells out to the house across the street A moment later in the doorway of the house directly across the street the boy appears

His son walks across the street as his father is watching the expression on the young man's face. He appears annoyed. The two shake hands. No hugs or warmth between them.

By this time Paula had divorced him and remarried still living in Compton while now on federal parole Johnny had acquired a two bed room home about a mile away one, that anyone else would have chosen to put a match to, but with the skills he had picked up in prison he had transformed the place into a fashionable piece of property

All the while Johnny was in prison his father kept in contact with his grandson having had taken him along with his other cousins across country to family reunions during the summer and fishing trips.

As his son grew older Johnny would write him letters and call him often on weekends something the boy looked forward to since the talk of the neighborhood ever since he was born was about his Dad who was a man you did not want to mess with.

The stories were told by the parents of his friends who personally knew Johnny before he was sent to federal prison stories that over the years fascinated the boy and he wanted to be just like him

When the boy turned seventeen he asked him what he thought about going to the military since Johnny's father older brother and twin all were in the Navy but not Johnny telling his only son

"Listen, if you want to see the world then get

You some money and go but I wouldn't sign up

To have some racist peckerwood kicking me

Like a dog. So no I wouldn't do it" End of conversation. What he didn't know was that his son was going through the usual teenage growing pains where they know everything and want to do whatever they want without being told No. He was looking to get away from his mother.

The boy had hoped his father would have something supportive to say about his idea but instead his father was totally against it to the point where he called it Voluntary Slavery, totally opposite of what he was told by his grandfather all those years Johnny was in prison.

When Johnny was in prison he only associated with the Con's who were doing time for having big money without fanfare or glamor. Soaking up everything he could that would prove to be crucial to his survival once he was back out on the streets. His marketability among the working class was limited to a degree. One thing he learned in prison was that he enjoyed working with his hands so he enrolled in a community college to learn auto mechanics along with body and fender.

Not so much with the intentions of getting a job but he would be able to work on his own vehicles and know everything about them from under the hood to the outside. However considering himself a jack of all trades but a master of none, Johnny along with another Hustler would do Industrial Burglaries taking nothing but a blank sheet of the payroll checks along with copies of the signatures. They would call in on the account to see what amount of cash the company has in the bank then send in a female to deposit the check in a fake checking account set up in advance

In addition on occasion he would sell ounces of cocaine to only a few selected people. Outside of that he was just in it for the money with no room for glory. The more glory the more worry about your name ringing at the police station a motto he lived by. Diversify keep it on the move because a moving target is harder to hit.

So engrossed with putting his life back together by nefarious tactics and criminal schemes he had no consciousness of mind to engage in family type of events, where before long his name was ringing at the federal building among the different parole agents who's clients would relay this information about him to get Snitch Brownie Points.

By now Paula was on her third husband and last he heard the boy had enlisted in the navy with the help of his grandfather things that never crossed his mind. Its like an "Out of sight Out of mind" type things not anything personal until someone else brings up the subject.

Johnny through all of his hustles decided to lease a Condo on the shores of the San Francisco Bay on the Island of Alameda. A third floor two bedroom two bath with fireplace overlooking the water and sky line of San Francisco off in the distance The location was perfect not all that far away from LA but far enough

More and more he found himself flying out of town to different States to case a possible pay day. A clear violation of his parole should he ever be arrested in another state without permission from his parole officer but it made no difference in his case because he had not reported in three whole years.

The way it worked is you had to give the feds a reason to look for you when you hung up the parole, outside of that they wait and allow you to bust yourself providing them with more to charge you with especially if it involved any type of police contact. The other is a technical violation that can carry up to eighteen months.

Within this time Johnny had learned through relatives that Paula had developed Alzheimer's and The Boy now a grown man had to move back home to Compton to take care of her. Trying to follow in his father' footsteps proved to be a bit too much for him when he was younger and it was through a cousin on Paula's side of the family who introduced the boy to barbering.

He had gotten so good at it that he was hired at a local college to teach classes He was on call for the television show TMZ to cut the hair of celebrities at three hundred dollars per head. Sometimes there would be an entire group like

The Beasty Boys there to do a segment that would amount to over a thousand dollar with tip for less than one hours work.

What Johnny had not realized was that over the years the admiration his son once had for him turned into a competitive resentment. The competitive part because he knew he could never be anything like his father and the resentment for not being in his life even though his mother had divorced him before he turned two years of age

It is quite possible that even his son had no idea of his own mental baggage at least he never outwardly displayed any form of animosity or ill feelings when he was in his presence.

One Saturday evening after just returning from a brisk walk out along the moon lit sky his son called him clearly distraught

"Pop I swear I don't know what to do it's getting so

I don't know how much more I can take"

"Slow down. What are you talking about?" directs his father

"Mom! I have to be up early three days a week

To teach a class, then I have to be gone some days

An she's out roaming lost in the street" sobs through the phone makes what he's saying almost unintelligible until Johnny commanded

"Hold on. Stop it! I'll be down there in a few days

I can help you out. Just chill out and stop

Acting like a Soft Touch"...

Johnny remembered when he was the same age He had not for one second of his life ever entertained the thought or possibility of being responsible for the health and welfare of his own mother therefore he had no concept of what the boy was feeling, taking into account too that the Paula Johnny knew was much different than the Mom his son knows

During his son's formative years of life Johnny was traveling up and down the California coast hustling. Absorbed in whatever project he was working on to increase his cash flow which meant he was chasing and casing Chasing a lead and casing a job that meaning it could involve just about anything.

Years passed. The once young and upcoming Hustler grew into a patient slow to anger and wiser older man. He recognized that when a person is talking to you that person is teaching you about who they are thus the cliché when you talk you teach when you listen you learn but when someone show's you who they are Believe them because actions always speak louder than words.

The telephone call from his son pleading for his help as his father did have an emotional effect on Johnny but at the same time he really had no desire to be around his ex, mainly because from personal experience with her he knew how manipulative she could be. Still his sole reason for even entertaining the idea was to help his son whom he had grown proud of that he did not choose to go down the path he had chosen.

Little did he realize that quite a lot had gone on in all those years he was up and down the highway and in prison Events that were thought of as Taboo and never talked about within the family Three weeks after that phone call Johnny rented a u-haul trailer loaded it with furniture and large mirrors His son suggested building a barber shop there in the garage so he would be able to stay home, work and take care of his mother at the same time A good idea and cost effective since Johnny was skilled in home building while in federal prison

Johnny also agreed to look after Paula when his son had to go teach a class or go on a job that took all day but he still did not trust her.

He made it a point every time he was left alone with her that he would record every second that she was in the same room as he

The very first day his son had to go to the college to teach a class leaving his dad there still working on the patio at the back of the house along with looking after his mother preparing meals for her. Paula came out into the patio where he was working as he quickly hit the record video on his phone unaware to her he was recording her

"What was that you said?" he asked her holding his phone slyly

"I said" she started slowly "I tried to keep everything

Together the best I could but are you back here to

Help me or for him?"

"Hold it!" he shot quickly "Let's get one thing straight I'm back here

For one reason only and that is to help the boy"

Clearly not the answer she was expecting and her facial expression told everything.

She was testing him to see if he too was sympathetic to her condition while in the days to follow she would test him again out in the garage where his son is cutting the hair of a neighbor The three men are all engaged in a conversation while she creeps out in the garage and takes a seat on the tan leather love seat Johnny brought from up north.

Paula invited herself into the conversation then acted as if she was going to dig her long finger nails into Johnny's arms because he would not go along with a story she was telling until Johnny said sternly

"Bitch you scratch me I'll break your jaw" she froze wide eyed and afraid until his son walked over taking her with his arm affectionately around her

"Come on Mom before he hurts you" and leads her into the house.

For the next six months she would keep her distance and stay in her room when he was there. As far as Johnny was concerned she was putting on an act for the purpose of getting her one and only to come back home to mommy. Johnny was not buying it

It was an early Monday morning when Johnny arrived at the house in Compton His son said he had an early class to teach and asked his Dad to come over early like he always does. Besides Johnny did enjoy having the opportunity to work with his son like normal father's do and teach him how to build and create with his hands but this day his son was not there

From the back yard which faced El Segundo the sound of automatic gun fire rings out followed by the exploding projectiles through the patio glass doors and walls of the house itself Johnny stands still listening watching feeling. Paula's screams echo from inside the house yet Johnny ignores her but instead makes his way carefully into the back yard to determine where the shots came from

The wooden fence was perforated with quarter size bullet holes. Johnny slid the gate back to see exactly when the gunfire started and stepped out on to El Segundo to estimate the carnage In bold red paint P E D O P H I L E was painted crudely across the fence along with the spent cartridge casings from the automatic weapon all on the ground

No other property was damaged. Johnny then went back into the house to call his son. First he thought to go check on Paula There she was in her bed the sheet red with her blood. He could see she was still alive but he was not of a mind to touch her instead he dialed 911 then as he was about to call his son Johnny hears his car pulling into the drive way unaware of what has just happened

Johnny goes to the front door and calls out to him

"Boy you better get in here Your mother's been shot" In a flash the younger version of Johnny races into the house to his mother's side She is breathing but not conscious. Holding her in his arms pleading

"Momma! Talk to me" In the distance outside the sound of sirens get closer until they are at the front door along with the Compton police

The paramedics had to forcefully separate the wounded woman from the clinging clutches of her son crying uncontrollably She is rushed to Martin Luther King hospital where she dies on the operating table.

After being questioned extensively by the police Johnny is told he is free to go while his son is an emotional wreck. The whole time his son was at the hospital with his mother Johnny stayed away since he felt absolutely nothing about her misfortune or her death.

When it came time for her service Johnny did not attend. His memories of her were anything but pleasant and he had no intentions of subjecting himself to sitting among a bunch of people caught up in Spook-ism lying about what a great and wonderful person she was.

As far as Johnny was concerned it was like the old female comedian back in the day Jackie Mom's Mabley use to joke

"They say you ain't suppose to say nothing about the dead unless you gone say something

Good. Well he dead. Good." Weeks later when he saw his father again he asked why he had not attended the service and Johnny replied

"That was your mother, not mine" not realizing that he was hurting his feelings especially since all of his life Johnny had told him

"If it hadn't been for Crown Royal and marijuana

You wouldn't be here" still his only son did not want to believe that his father could be so heartless as not to be there at least for him Something that not once ever crossed his mind which should have been plain and clear to his son.

One day the two of them, father and son were working out in the patio just about finishing up. He and his son sat talking smoking a Blunt as Johnny shared with him stories about his life when he was living in Chicago and how virtually everything in his past, the home caught fire and was burned to the ground. The catholic school and church he attended was demolished to discover skeletons of deceased infants found buried where the nun's convent once stood.

His son stated,

"Then you can say that this is where your life

Actually began and you know you'll always have

Some place to go" and Johnny replies

"Yeah to Jail" his son thinking it was a joke. But it wasn't.

He had not ever considered that house as his home. Since he had no emotional ties to Paula or anything about what she provided for him When Paula met Johnny in prison he was a virtual restless spirit but he was always open with her about who he was and what his intentions were when he got out.

Hoping to influence his decision Paula bought the house a car and two complete Wardrobe' of men clothes and only asked that he be there.

It would not ever be enough because he did not want it from the start most importantly he didn't want her.

Life Goes On

In 2013 Johnny was discharged from federal parole after a series of technical violations but no police contact. He took up residence in the city of Gardena in 2016, only minutes away from where his son was still living in Compton. Since the passing of Paula his relationship with the boy was virtually nonexistent. Through no choice of his own, but his son was crushed by the passing of his mother while it meant nothing to his father.

Ever since the day of the shooting Johnny has felt like there was more to it than just some random act. But other than that it was just a feeling he was not able to shake. It seemed with the death of his mother the boy allowed his true feelings about his father to be known. He hated his father for not being in his life and now that his mother was gone he knew not to expect too much of anything from the man he admired but hated at the same time.

Being raised by his mother and a variety of three different men, two she married, men who she dominated and clearly had no respect for judging by the way she would not only verbally abuse them, she would physically abuse them with vicious slaps in the face and locking them out of the house after forcing them to pay whatever bills that needed to be paid. His son along with one of his friends in their Teens actually beat up one man she married name Bill and he had to be hospitalized. Once released from his injuries he went right back to the house.

Being raised by his mother he was not without male influence, however observing the manner in which his mother reacted to the men sent him the wrong messages as he was growing up. But Johnny was not of a mind to do any Babysitting at this late stage in life. Not even for the twin grandsons his son attempted to tell him about via a text while his father answered the text with

"Don't name those MF's after me!" That was close to Two years ago and he did not even know their names. The only thing he knew was he would not be able to overlook what he knew to be true nor did he have the slightest desire to.

It did not matter to Johnny that this was his first born child, his son who would ultimately carry on his name. What mattered was the boy had

Reality and Fantasy confused something that Johnny realized in his son but felt it was not his place to making any attempts at directing him when he was not there for him during his formative years. His son made a mistake one day that more or less sealed his father's decision to simply walk away rather than go through the waste of thought energy and possibly running the risk of having to do something very drastic.

At Sixty-five years of age Johnny had no desire to spend what few years he had remaining on the planet going back to re-establish anything that he deemed as over and done. Including trying to fix what he had no hand in breaking between himself and his son. Instead he focused on avoiding drama. Life is too short for that. Peace and fifty feet was all he needed. Social distancing only calls for six.

Every morning before the sun rises Johnny is at the gym working out. It was his source of stress release and it kept him healthy. Initially he had been working out with weights on and off since he was sixteen years old and always maintained a healthy lifestyle. His cocaine snorting days were long gone although he still liked his Scotch.

When Johnny was the age of 60 he realized that he could not continue to do the same things he had done all his life and expect a different result. No matter how bad he wanted to have a family life still he had no idea how to go against his own character and pretend everything was fine when it wasn't. Faking was a characteristic that he was not in any way familiar with.

The thought had crossed his mind to make an attempt at mending the fences between himself and his son but fully understanding the mind of a now grown man raised and influenced solely by a demented woman with ideals and principals that only a desperate person would put up with was more than enough reason for Johnny to keep his distance for the sake of avoiding an event like the one that happened to the late entertainer Marvin Gay.

The Wake Up

She was known as the Gun Lady. Ghost Guns were Glock Guns that were being assembled and sold legally. She would purchase the parts for two hundred fifty dollars then sell the completed fully functioning weapon for twenty-five hundred. Born in Oakland in 1975 Reba is her name a young woman who clearly missed her calling in life and needed to be on the cover of Vogue Magazine

Kenny Gales told Johnny about Reba They attended high school at the same time and over the years they stayed in contact. Reba was the mother of two young children. Shawn her son 20 and Tasha her daughter 22 Although Reba was born in Oakland she was raised by a single parent, a mother who was an A T and T Executive and traveled the country on special assignments that would take her to places like Chicago New Jersey Indianapolis even China.

While her mother was busy with her job, Reba had to take on the responsibility of looking after her older brother Phillip, even though he was a year older than Reba he clearly was his mother's child. Reba on the other hand was more independent and responsible. The type of men she attracted, large scale drug dealers Cocaine and Heroin and even though her mother made certain that her children wanted for nothing, Reba had a mind of her own and was wise way beyond her age

She had to be. Her brother had gotten a taste of Heroin at the age of 19 and she made it her mission to look after him. Coming up he was big for his age and likeable by everyone. But once that "Dog Food" takes over Your life is no longer yours. You belong to the Drug Dealer.

Johnny had gotten information on a coin dealer who sold kilo's of cocaine but he would need a weapon because from what he knew of the middle age white man, not only did he sell the cocaine but he used it and was paranoid. Johnny had to drive to Oakland from Los Angeles to meet with Reba since he did not discuss business over the phone.

Reba lived in the Diamond District of Oakland and her job was actually managing three apartment buildings for the co-operation she worked for out of San Francisco. The Ghost gun assembly and sales was simply a hobby that she turned into a lucrative side line business.

The first time they met there was something electric that generated between them. Nothing sexual, but something more than that and she felt it too. Back during the 1970's when he was living in Oakland there were a number of women Johnny had been with intimately and her

Mother was one of those women. Twice she had gotten pregnant by Johnny but did not tell him knowing that during that stage of his life he was not the parenting type but she liked him. Johnny was under the impression that Philip was the son from her previous marriage while now as a young man he looked more like Johnny, he lived in Florida

"You don't remember my momma do you

Ruby was her name and she use to tell me

Stories about you"

"Oh. really?" He countered while she went into her purse to produce a photograph of her mother on her phone.

"This is her" holding the phone in front of him At first glance he remembered her right off

"Yes I do remember her!" switching his eyes back to Reba as his mind back tracks through time Was it possible she may be his daughter. The resemblance was mirror like close. The same nose complexion and an attitude that said "I'm not the one to play with" Just like Johnny

"Where is your mother now, still in Oakland?" he asked

"No, she passed away last year in Florida.

She was staying with Phillip"

"Sorry to hear that" he offered and she was genuinely appreciative.

"Okay, did she tell you who your father is?" he asked

"Not directly but she did tell me that when

I do meet him I'll know it" Between them both it was obvious. No need for a DNA the evidence was in their spirits He wrapped his arms around his daughter and savored the feeling of being a proud father. It wasn't the same feeling as with his son that was an accident. But Ruby was more to his liking. She was easy going and down to earth taking care of her elderly mother as well. Reba was in fact named after her late pistol toting grandmother

Once they got past recognizing who they were to each other they talked about the business at hand where without question he takes out his wallet and gives her five hundred dollars to construct his Tool. She already had one put together, a twenty-five hundred dollar gun but said

"All I pay is two fifty for the parts this is five-" attempting to give him half of it back but he tells her to keep it.

He asks her,

"So where are my grandchildren?" She told him that she had gotten them an apartment in one of the buildings she managed on 98th Ave in Oakland Tasha worked part time while Shawn was working on his music

Johnny assured her that as soon as he concluded this last piece of business he wanted to spend more time with them all together which brought her close to tears hearing him say that.

Like her father she wasn't one for displaying her emotions easily. Because of her brother Philip and his drug use she had to be hard in dealing with him, along with Deacon, a former male friend she had been with for seven years and was like a father figure to both children. He never allowed the children to see him use. Yet it got to be too much for Reba who on two separate occasions had to virtually save his life from ingesting massive amounts of cocaine.

For a woman she was by no means a Soft Touch.

The Lick

George Dennis owned and operated a rare coin store specializing in the condition quality and age of coins he bought and sold. Located in the heart of downtown Los Angeles on James Wood and 6th street making it impossible to avoid being recorded on any one of the hundreds of security cameras stationed practically on every building within one hundred feet of the other

COVID 19 made it easy since masks were mandatory and having been through the legal system Johnny knew to also conceal his ears which too could be used as another form of identification when compared from surveillance footage he was wearing a pair of wireless head-phones

The first thing he did was establish an escape route. The on ramp leading to three different freeways was close. The Harbor 110 the 5 and the 101

Wearing an Adidas Tiro warm up suit with matching gym shoes he walks up to the door and has to be buzzed in from the inside.

The store owner is standing behind the counter wearing a holstered 9. Millimeter on his side a clear message that he would use lethal force to protect his property

From the ceiling supported by two steel cables hung behind the counter was a huge confederate flag. Security cameras captured everything and no doubt a direct connection to the police department. With his gun concealed in the back of his pants Johnny produces a 1801 Morgan silver dollar under the pretense of wanting to sell it. It was fake

The instant the owner lowered his eyes to examine the coin, Johnny struck him viciously in the head with the butt of the Glock knocking him to the floor leaping over the counter to quickly disarm the dazed man

Johnny forces the gun in his mouth shattering two front teeth saying

"Three seconds from being a dead man.

The cocaine and the money Three Two-" before the count of one the man points to where it could be found. Conscious of the time he forces the man to open the safe where he finds a Kilo of cocaine and Seventy-Thousand dollars in cash then smashes him in the head with the gun one last time knocking him out cold. In under three minutes Johnny is out and undetected on the freeway.

The one thing on his mind now was getting to know the Daughter he didn't know he had. His grandchildren Tasha and Shawn He was in fact excited at the idea of being a grandfather Having grown up in what he considered as madness he felt it would be a welcoming experience to try something different with people and not feel it necessary to always be on guard

Old habits die hard but during the entire time he was on the freeway he made a vow to himself that he would not run the risk of working another Lick taking the chance of being arrested or killed, something that had not mattered to him ever before.

Everything was different now He was a four time grandfather yet two of them he would never know because he did not have the slightest inclination to have anything to do his son who was now a grown man with character flaws his father did not approve of. Flaws that under other circumstances would cost his son his life

Instead Johnny chose to sever his ties with him completely. He actually had no feelings what so ever about his decision to walk away. No anger or sadness in the least. A choice he made for his own peace of mind It was easy for Johnny because, there were never any emotional ties from the very beginning or sense of family like he felt when he met his daughter Reba. The holiday season was rapidly approaching and he wanted for the first time in his life to share Christmas with his Family

It was a time of the year that meant nothing to him since he was a child From January to October life at home was like having to walk barefoot on razor blades making certain not to ruffle the feathers of the fire breathing dragon called mother. Although not the same for his siblings who seem to always be in good graces with her something as a child he did not understand. He only knew that he was Different.

No longer a young man his stamina may have slowed down but not his mindset. Although he had taught himself to think first even though he had grown out of reacting instead of acting, people around him that were now required to wear face masks due to the pandemic suddenly found a sense of courage from their faces being hidden and were quick to shout out racial slurs especially from the safety of a moving vehicle.

In the stores he notices how it was mostly women who were quick to harass anyone they encountered not wearing a face mask. Johnny always wore one out in public for his own protection as well as for others but mostly to prevent anyone from making the mistake of saying anything to him for his character would always be the same.

No longer hot tempered but more lethal when faced with hostility. Self -Preservation comes first. With six inch case knife in hand he would hit one time in the solar plexus then walk away leaving the lifeless body where it created the altercation. Peaceful by Will but violent by nature

Because of the pandemic people were urged not to travel over five hundred miles or would have to be quarantined for fourteen days if they did. Johnny would facetime his daughter and grandchildren often.

At the beginning of this health alert he thought it was fine especially since there was no one in his life he wanted to be with, other than an occasional visit to see his sister Regina in San Jose along with his two nephews Carl and John. But with this new discovery life has taken on a whole different meaning.

The Reason

East Oakland was known as a rough and violent area. 98th avenue was the street where one of the apartments Reba managed is located an area dominated by drug addicts and the homeless a place most women dare not to venture at night alone. But not Reba She had rules that the tenants as well as the homeless hanging around the building had to follow or suffer the consequences

There was one homeless dope fiend that she had told on a number of occasions not to sleep in the trash bin area, yet he had taken a mattress blocking the bin door where the tenants were complaining and afraid to confront the man until Reba with one of her Glock Pistols sent him running out into the street without looking and he is hit by a speeding car breaking a leg and his right arm. Needless to say after recovering from his injuries he never returned to that building. Yes, without even knowing it she was truly her father's Daughter.

Reba told her father that she had found his son on social media and had been following him for a few years Knowing now that he was in fact her brother she wanted to meet him in person with the hidden hope that the two would reconcile.

What she didn't know was reconciliation was not an option with her father. He had strict rules he lived by assuring her that he had no problem with her getting to know his son, but not to expect him to alter his decision to have anything to do with him.

Respecting his wishes was not an issue as she Tasha and Shawn were aware that this now her brother and their uncle under no possible circumstances would ever again in life be allowed within arm's length of his father The disdain between the two of them was deeper than anyone would ever know.

The truth be told he knew that his son was a pedophile. A predator that would not stand a chance in prison but would be abused tortured and often found left brutally murdered in a prison cell by men who had families, wives and daughters. This was the reason why there could be no reconciliation

Sure it was his blood which meant absolutely nothing to Johnny since he knew how your own blood could turn out to be your worse enemy. Logic is what ruled and directed him. Not emotions. Still Reba was hopeful

His reasons for not telling her everything was he wanted her to discover it on her own since Johnny was certain that like a leopard can't change its spots, nor was it possible for a pedophile to change its habits.

People only do what they know so clearly this was something that was taught to him from a very young age, but when he got to the age where he was able to talk she stopped but too late because the act was already embedded in his mind. She even had a tattoo put on the left side of her back to commemorate their sexual involvement, something as a professed Christian was against her religion.

None of it mattered especially since there was no possible way for any of it to be undone. Johnny only wanted to distance himself from what he felt was a killing offense since among his own sisters he learned that an uncle had molested not one but three of his sisters when he was in Chicago living with them. This was revealed when Johnny was in his early 30's after the uncle responsible had died from natural causes.

Just as well. Had Johnny known anything about it the uncle would have been punished mercilessly until he was dead

Old School Crew

The clock on the gym wall read 5:30 a.m. when his ear buds alerted a call coming in. It was Reba

"Pop! Shawn been kidnapped"

"What" her Father blurted out

"They busted into the apartment I got them

In one of the buildings I manage on 98th. Tasha said it was three of them who was trying to take her but Shawn fought them off her then they all teamed up on him. Tasha ran to get help" screaming bleeding from a broken champagne bottle she broke over the head of one assailant but cutting her hand in the process along with possible broken ribs from fighting with her would be abductors but was successful in getting away now being kept in the hospital over night for further observation.

Donald Rae through his contacts learned that the gang was part of a crew from Los Angeles, a place where his grandson had never been. Since Johnny lives in LA Donald Rae relays what he uncovered assuring him

"Man you know if you need me it ain't nothin' but a word I'll keep digging on this end"

Many years before Donald Rae and Johnny found themselves in the federal penitentiary at the same time where life is only worth a carton of cigarettes or less. Johnny got involved with a drug deal and a con who turned out be a Rat, thinking that he would impress Johnny by asking him to hold seven hundred dollars cash for him. It was money from drugs the snitch was forced to smuggle in by two killers.

Twice the snitch asked Johnny to stash money in his cell for him, the second time Johnny stiffed the guy telling him the guards searched his cell found the money hidden inside a picture frame but kept it only returning the picture frame Needless to say, the two Killers were not going for the game and wanted their money back.

As far as Johnny was concerned the problem was not his since he got the money from the Rat therefore the two guys could not say anything directly to him. Johnny had gone to Donald Rae seeking a Plug on some weed to sell giving him part of the money to purchase the product.

Both Donald Rae and Johnny were in the Band room inside the gym where they had been smoking the merchandise. Donald Rae had a Bass Guitar sent in and was learning how to play it when both killers walked in and stationed themselves at the entrance.

Immediately Johnny notices them while Donald Rae is oblivious since he had no idea of what happened. The smoke was good as Donald Rae plucked the strings on his instrument. No doubt the two men were packing. Johnny nonchalantly says to Donald Rae,

"I need you to go find Punchie and tell him

To send me a knife"

"Awe Man you trippin" laughing heartily until Johnny says

"No. Some drama is about jump off. Seriously" Without another word he puts his guitar down and leaves the band room, while Johnny and the two killers are on opposites sides of the room sit watching the other. Minutes later Donald Rae returns walking swiftly past the two men posted on both sides of the entrance back to Johnny and slips him the knife without being seen. Johnny then says to his friend,

"Now you go head this is going to get ugly"

"Oh hell naw!" Donald Rae replies picking up a Drum clamp clinched in his fist

"Whatever it is we ridding this together"

"You see Buck and Big Moe over there. I want you to walk out ahead of me past them I got it just watch my back". Knowing the reputation of the two men Donald Rae does as he is asked.

Their prison instincts let them know that Johnny too now has a weapon and just as Donald Rae is about to pass them both men retreat. That day was the beginning of a lifelong friendship.

What He did not know was if the connection was Reba. Her social media account contained all of her personal information including names of family members. Someone was cyber stalking her but was mistaken about exactly where she lived. Johnny had a nagging thought in the back of his mind that something more sinister was taking place.

He had no unresolved Beefs with anyone male or female in Los Angeles since he did not allow issues to exist in his life but always addressed them as they developed. His main concern now was finding out where and who had taken his grandson, while the trail from the Bay to LA was a lot of ground to cover

Johnny called Reba back

"I need you to think. Who do you know here in

Los Angeles who might be capable of doing

Something like this?"

She stops to think for a moment then says

"I have a few social media friends who live in

LA but never met personally like your son"

"No online hook ups or guys hitting on you?" he asks his daughter

"None" she answers "I'm always straight forward about that I don't mislead men on line because I know how that can go"

"Was Shawn in a gang?"

"No" Reba answered "The only thing he was involved in

Was making Beats with his friends"

"Ok, let me call a friend in Oakland but I'm

On top of it"

Johnny makes a call to Donald Rae in Oakland the one person if anyone with the resources to uncover who is responsible.

Johnny face times Reba who is at the apartment on 98th Broken furniture and glass The door smashed in Speaking to her father,

"Pop this don't make no sense"

"Just take a deep breath and as soon as I hear back

From my people I'll be in touch" the screen goes black

Reba paces the empty disheveled apartment with Glock in one hand and cell phone in the other not really knowing what to do except do as her father instructed and stay calm. Still the Oakland police have not shown up.

Forty-five minutes later Shawn came bursting through the door with two men chasing behind him. Reba is standing in the middle of the floor when she raises the gun and fires two rounds past Shawn both shots hit one man in the face while the other turns and runs away. With his hair all over his head clothes torn and bloody he appeared to be in good health. The man on the floor is dead.

A Mother protecting Her Son was front page news of the Oakland tribune She made it a point to call her father before he saw it on the evening news, in fact she had him on the phone during the entire interview she had with the police about the kidnap and shooting.

As it turned out the dead guy was part of a group who also made Beats but Shawn with his crew were creating competition all the way to LA

One thing was for certain Reba knew her children and had no sense of fear when it came to protecting them. But this was the first time she ever killed anyone realizing after it was over that she felt nothing, not even a hint of sorrow for the man she shot. The owners of the co-operation unanimously decided to promote her to Chief of Security with her own office car and driver.

The only Hero in her life was her Mother, as far as bringing her into the world and providing for her single handedly. Other than that it was Reba who had to take on her mother's role at an early age looking after her older brother along with her aging grandmother leaving no room for much of anything else between them as far as warmth. Reba was taught how to be hard yet a woman at the same time. Most men make the mistake of considering a woman as the weaker sex, when the truth is the pain they experience at child birth would kill a man because a man was not created to reproduce only to fertilize

Having her father in her life now seemed to strengthen her, made her feel not so much alone since her mother had passed away.

Life Changes

The Mead co-operation was a company composed of men with real estate holdings throughout the entire San Francisco Bay Area. Until Reba brought attention to the conditions of the building on 98th

It was big news around the Bay. She was all over Instagram and Twitter as

"Gun Lady Oakland's own Have Gun Will Use It", mimicking the old TV western Have Gun Will Travel. She was given a budget that she used to have security cameras installed in all the stairwells the elevator repaired along with the door intercom connected and able to be activated from each apartment.

Her position required her to have a car and driver. His name was Kurt Six foot one with long dreads a former gang member who decided to turn his life around for the sake of his three year old daughter since the child's mother was hopelessly addicted to crack cocaine.

He acquired the job through an At Risk Program being no stranger to a life of violence and the criminal justice system. Kurt had been her driver going on three weeks where he would drive his own car to her office to switch to the company Lincoln Navigator. From day one it was clear there was an attraction between the two and while Reba made it plain that she did not mix business with pleasure Kurt was enamored by her.

She was so elegant and graceful on top of being recognized as a force to be reckoned with made him speak his mind letting her know that at some point there was going to be some sparks flying between them. It was just a matter of when. From his rearview mirror he can see her smiling not knowing that her thoughts were on what she would do after hours.

In the short period of time she learned about the situation with his daughter. A soft spot in her heart that would lead to more than he ever expected For the most part he was a decent man while he found himself the subject of jealousy within the circle of associations he had in his life. Reba would change that.

Kurt had an issue with being accepted. clearly a sign of what he lacked during his formative years but the longer he was around Reba she was actually teaching him life lessons without realizing it. Their relationship developed into a serious affair to the point where they ended up living together. Even though he made it clear that he entertained a number of different women one thing he did not do was allow any of them to be in her presence with disrespect, not that Reba would allow it.

Many of his so called friends were actually jealous of him being with a successful slightly older woman. Not only was she beautiful but she had an imagination that went further than any form of intelligence he had ever seen or known drawing him closer and closer to her. It was her true spirit her Energy

There were weekends when Johnny would drive up from Los Angeles and visit with Reba Kurt Shawn Tasha and Kurt's three year old little girl The group of them all together gave their Grandfather a feeling he had never felt in his entire life although he would not let it be known simply in words alone

Even Kurt at times reminded him of himself when he was in his late 20's Only difference was Johnny did not belong to a gang other than a gang of Dames who would fan the same flame at the end of a pistol just like he did.

Now in the autumn of his years he finds that through his daughter he is learning about the real meaning of family instead of what it is like to be in the company of people claiming to be family yet you are constantly on high alert ready to take arms in hand at any second.

When from outside the sound of an explosion shakes the building and rattles the windows Seconds later another explosion the sound of a hovering helicopter outside. Reba grabs her pistol Johnny rushes to the front window to see the streets filled with masked people bashing car windows throwing rocks at occupied homes moving up the street like an ocean wave. Kurt rushes the baby to a closet as Tasha and Shawn hit the floor

Both Reba and Johnny guns drawn take up position ready to stop what or whoever comes through that front door. Tossing her father another clip

Was it a Riot or a Purge although the sound of the chopper outside had grown distant it could still be heard following the massive crowd down the street Shawn turns on the TV to see the news. It was everywhere going on all over the city. A number of different groups targeting certain neighborhoods dominated by certain ethnic groups with the intentions of starting a race war

Once the baby is secure with Tasha Kurt returns with a gun of his own Shawn follows him with a steel baseball bat ready to smash some heads More so it was the excitement with having his grandfather there since this is one young man who will avoid a confrontation at all cost, until the other person charges too much.

"What do we do now?" Kurt asks Johnny

"We don't do nothing unless one of those

Clowns come through that door, so we can relax" evaluating Reba as she is clearly weighing the situation for herself who too agrees but keeps her gun close by.

"I think we all ought to stay inside for a bit" Reba suggests,

"At least until we know exactly what's going on" The cell phones begin to ring first Reba then Johnny Donald Rae is on the phone

"Man you seeing this! You still in the Bay?"

"Yeah I'm with my daughter and grandkids"

"Everybody alright"

"Yeah we good how bout you"

"Man you know I'm way up here in these hills and not likely they'll make it this far"

Donald Rae explained how the flash waves of violence is nothing but the government attempting to start civil unrest so they can declare Marshall Law Ask why the police on the ground or the helicopter not once made an attempt to contain or disburse the crowd claiming to be monitoring the situation because they are the ones behind it.

But the NFAC had a different idea. Not only were they trained ex-army soldiers. There were members within the infrastructure secretly placed in congress long in advance knowing from history that the government would in fact attempt to convert to a dictatorship. The Black Panther Party back in 1965 made a monumental difference with influencing politicians to change certain laws virtually overnight Not much has changed since then depending on how you look at it.

Donald Rae concludes the call,

"Man I got to check back on my twin grand boys but if you need me for anything just holler" the line goes dead

Lady Of The House

The Good Ole Boys movement was taking on momentum even within major police stations all across the country making it difficult for law enforcement to know where or who to target. Not everyone in blue uniforms shared the same ideals as some of their brother officers who were a small secret group scattered across the country

In the meantime on Capital Hill in Washington D.C. a bill has been placed before congress separating the entire Southern States of the country as payment for the "Forty Acers And A Mule" that was never paid to the former Slaves considering the Holocaust Victims Japanese and other victimized cultures were compensated and are still being to this day while one race of people have not.

Ever since the Gun Lady incident Reba had gained an enormous amount of attention and popularity. Throughout the social media, publicity from

Nationwide news coverage of the event tragic as it was, still Reba directed the focus where it should be during her interviews with the press speaking her mind unaware that the whole nation was listening to her. It was as if her life was taking on a direction of its own one that she had no real desire to entertain. Politics, but as she would say to her father in the face of a dilemma

"Let um bring it on I ain't no punk" She had a spirit and energy that told her she could do anything she wanted to as long as she put her mind to it. The home she lived in on Diamond Ave. just below the Mormon Temple predominantly affluent blacks and Asians was why that wave of violence swept down her street

Could it have been part of a much bigger plan since where she lived was no secret. History has shown that if the President of the United States can be killed, a mere public activist like Doctor Martin Luther King Nipsey Hussle or Reba would be no problem.

But Johnny had always been a conscious observer of everything going on around him recognizing the growth of his daughter's popularity

He was taking note of the people in her inner circle. It was his parental nature to protect her knowing all too well how the people closest to you can be the ones to do you the most harm.

Between her two children Tasha was the adventurist tiny in size but large in curiosity. The jet setter displaying the face of an angle for the unknowing to covet until she flipped into business mode advising her would be suitors that

Romance without finance was a nuisance and she had bills to pay. She had no children of her own and enjoyed life to the fullest. For the most part her best game was the truth which she had no conscious of mind to conceal. Shawn on the other hand is easy going Laid back and difficult to bring to anger. But once he goes there he becomes silent lethal and unpredictable.

Trusting his instincts was all he knew to do especially now he was paying close attention to everything since it pertained to the life of the one person in his entire life who gave him the sense of Family The one

Person he would give his life for without a thought. More than anything she had given him a sense of belonging.

The days turned into weeks then months. The Nation of Islam along with N.F.A.C. both pledged their services providing her with security.

Kurt was no stranger to violence having grown up on the streets of San Francisco being raised by a single parent. In a lot a ways he reminded Johnny of himself when he was that age the only difference was Johnny never belong to a gang. Johnny could see how Reba made a difference in his life all for the good. She took on the responsibility of raising his daughter when the child's birth mother chose Crack Cocaine.

Reba added substance to his life. A direction something that he had not ever known other than abiding by the rules within the gang he had been in who all for the most part were envious of him something Kurt was not able to see until she pointed it out where once he saw it for himself he chose the direction as a responsible young father instead.

They were in fact a family. Johnny was elated at the idea of being a grandfather. This type of lifestyle he always figured was for Squares who worked a nine to five paid their taxes and a registered voter. Not so...

Call it tunnel vision, an inability to see past the words in order to grasp the understanding. Or was there another term some mental disorder gone undiagnosed. All the same the only thing he did know to do was follow his instincts which he did when it came to just about every aspect of life.

It was via a Twitter post when Johnny learned back in Los Angeles on the corner where he held a residence the police killed a local Hispanic Man for breaking into a home. His instincts were telling him there was

More to it than what the news reported.

Ever since the kidnapping of newspaper Heir Patty Hearst from her Berkeley apartment in 1973 the Department of justice established a task force designed specifically to maintain surveillance on paroled Bank Robbers believed to be still active.

In the summer of 1974 there was a gun fight in Compton between the FBI and the Symbionese Liberation Army the group believed to be an organization ran by a black man name Donald Defreeze responsible for kidnapping Patty Hearst. This same task force received information that Johnny was still active but not entirely true.

Banks had gotten to be too risky while drug dealers could not call the police yet his name kept popping up in the investigations causing the task force to keep him on the radar. Someone was deliberately making him a target for the department of justice.

Many of the guys Johnny had known from federal prison thought he had grown paranoid about the task force until the same two guys from Lompoc federal prison were killed in a bank hold up by special agents who had been following them for months then executed them on their way out of the bank. All the while Johnny was in Oakland with his daughter so were they.

It Never Rains

Now back in Los Angeles the first thing he looked for was the small piece of clear tape he always left stuck to the door as he entered as a sign if anyone had entered while he was away. The tape was gone but he continued on realizing that he is possible being watched. The years he spent in federal prison he watched listened and learned the ways of the D.O.J. and how they operate.

In the garage of his Condo he kept a Black and Gray 1985 customized Cadillac Se Ville on Vogues. Carefully he examined the garage searching for any sign of a bug. With keys in his right hand he pops the automatic trunk to examine its contents. Nothing appears disturbed. This is where he kept large sums of cash on hand since he rarely drove the car.

Instead he preferred the 1977 Gold Se Ville on Vogues which too has been fully restored It was something about those old Cadillac's he just could not get away from.

During his youth it was not wise to hit a lick then run to the Cadillac dealer drawing attention to yourself. But now in the autumn of his years whenever the police see him always dressed in a two or three piece suit with a neatly trimmed beard of white they pay him no attention because of his age. These LA cops mostly target young Black men something he discovered years before on a fluke when speeding down an alley near 79th and Mc Kinley in east LA driving a customized Mercedes with an ounce of heroin and a gun in the car, in addition to being on the run from federal parole.

Hard to believe it had been seven years since he has been off of federal parole.

During the week Johnny drove a leased Nissan SUV more so because it attracted less to no attention. The sun was just setting in the sky when clearly two unmarked police cars about to enter the front electric gate. Why they were entering the building he had no idea. Having secured his condo before leaving it One Cadillac was in the garage the gold one was under a tarp clear on the other side of the complex.

Not that the police had any reason to come looking for him, since the last bank he robbed was close to thirty years ago. Statute of limitations played out before half the cops on duty were even in high school. Still he had to be sure they were now looking for him. His outside parking allowed him a clear view of the front door of his unit. All four officers converge on the spot directly next door where a shot caller gang member resides with his girl.

Johnny starts the vehicle and just as he is about to exit the front gate the entire ground shakes from the force of the explosion that came from the direction of his spot. Uncertain of what was happening he pulled outside the gate parked down the street and walked quickly back inside the complex.

Someone had entered one of the center units, broken a natural gas line from the wall placed a flat cookie pan covered with steel eating utensils and a plastic bottle of lighter fluid inside a microwave, demolishing an entire side of the building. Inside the courtyard Military helicopters flew low overhead three in a pattern. Flood lights from the choppers blanket the early night sky along with the sound of the whirling blades keeping the craft in the air All over the news the story of the White House being taken over A woman protester being shot to death senators being rushed to safety This was the rebellion that had been boiling over but had now come to a head. He thought about his daughter realizing that if this was going to get worse at least she has a good security team.

The "Good Ole Boy's" had sparked a movement that was similar to the Gestapo of Hitler's army. The entire country is divided politically and morally. Like certain federal agents who don't believe certain ex-felons should be allowed to live. These were the agents who formed a task force specifically for that purpose and it seem that now the entire country had a green light to kill

One of those agents was once a parole agent who had Johnny assigned to his caseload and soon realized that the parolee spent most of his time between the law library and the weight room almost cost the agent his career when Johnny secretly recorded the agent making incriminating statements. Having been demoted because of this ex-con he would have his justice

The whole time he was concerned with his daughter becoming the target of violence not once did he consider that he might be instead.

His son had obtained a certain degree of recognition in his community as being a role model for the youth and was even given a government grant for providing a place for children to go after school It was his barber shop where he had a special room set up in the back for the children.

Totally unaware that his son a now full grown man in his 50's has a seething hatred for him Hate stimming from his youth when Johnny was not in his life a time when he so desperately needed him to be. But that hate turned to fear when years later he confessed to Johnny that he had molested his step-daughter when she was fourteen asking about the statute of limitations and his fear of being exposed by his father. All of this is fueled by the news reports and social media postings with his daughter made him heartlessly jealous because he was the first to be born not her it was no fault of his own causing him to set out on a mission to destroy his father for destroying his life.

It was as if the entire nation was preparing for Civil War stimming from the atrocities being committed within the White House Rioters being shot dead as they vandalize the white house property breaking down doors smashing windows stealing documents from the desk assaulting the police. Across the entire nations in mostly small city's violence has reached record high numbers against people of color resulting into violent clashes ending with the loss of life and property.

Since the beginning of the disturbance Johnny kept in contact with his daughter by text or Facetime at least once a day assuring himself that she is in fact safe and secure, while at the same time he is providing her with peace of mind so not to worry about him. Even though she grew up without him in her life she held no blame or judgement but was only glad to finally have her father in her life. He chose to drive his Gold 77 Se Ville since it had been a good while since he had been in it but it was his favorite along with it being the year his daughter was born. She let him know that she was concerned about his drinking so much too.

Having made the decision to ease up on the Scotch he drove over to the cannabis spot on Compton and Santa Fe. Parked across the street he noticed the same unmarked police car with only one occupant on the driver's side. He steps out of his vehicle with walking stick in his right hand walking towards the corner making the face more visible.

Sure it had been a while but one thing he never forgot was a face. No matter how much time had passed since he actually saw the person the image is locked in his mind. This was no exception as his thoughts did like a lap top and there it was his old parole agent continuing to walk as if he saw nothing.

He was only in the store ten minutes. When he came out the car was gone. Coincidence It did not feel that way walking back to the car. In the middle of the street he made a U-turn heading back towards Figueroa all the while watching his rear view mirror before Redondo Beach Blvd police lights flash behind him from the unmarked car.

From the squad car loud speaker he is ordered to exit the car all the while Johnny is dialing 911 on his cell phone not responding to the commands. The city of Compton no longer has a

Police Department, it has The Sherriff's Office and they do not operate alone.

Johnny pulled the gold classic Cadillac into the McDonald's parking lot there on the corner of Figueroa and Redondo Beach Blvd,

"Nine one, one" the operator sang

"My name is John Collier and I'm being victimized by some guy waving a gun having road rage" Johnny quickly reported and within minutes the Carson division had dispatched three two maned vehicles.

Only then did Johnny step out of the car with his hands raised. Two of the newly arrived officer's hand cuffed Johnny walking him to their squad car. In turning around he was able to see his old parole officer talking with what looks like the Sargent judging by the stripes on his uniform. The man appears to be annoyed as Johnny sits in the back of the police car unable to hear what was being said.

Instead he sat quietly watching everything going on around him. Slowly one by one the police cars began driving away leaving the Sargent and the old PO. The person to return to Johnny was the officer who was driving the squad car. He let Johnny out removed the handcuff saying

"It turned out to be a mistake and you're free to go". The truth be told had he not made the 911 call he surely would have been killed. More than just racial it was political where the mentality had gone back to 1812. The Militia was what this country was born and raised on only in this day and age it has a different name. Fortunate as it was the Sargent knew the old Agent personally along with him being a part of a special squad which he did not and wanted nothing to do with. Throughout the whole incident Johnny never saw his son parked down the street watching.

With the condition the country was presently in he knew it would be a total waste of time and money to retain any lawyer to Sue, so there was only one thing left to do. Strap Up and take no hostages The homeland terrorist have decided to take off their hooded sheets to make it plain and clear this is a War On Nationwide television having taken over Capitol Hill a clear insurrection.

A Change Is Coming

The entire nation was nervous as whores in church not knowing who was a Good Ole Boy hiding behind a badge or just a coward driving down the street shooting at innocent people. Having to wear face masks gave certain people the courage to act out their hostility they otherwise would not exhibit for fear of being identified.

Too late to get scared now not that it would do any good. Only thing to do is abide by the first law of nature with a little bible scripture added to it, go about your own business and take your Social Distancing to fifty feet instead of six.

His choice of weapon is a Smith & Wesson 38. Which he carried in a clip holster at the small of his back His social life consisted of the gym in the morning The remainder of his days usually spent following the Stock market keeping track of his investments or working on one of his two classic Cadillacs or writing poetry A form of therapy he took up in prison.

Better to express it on paper than to physically express a hostile poem in the direction from which the inspiration was developed. Still keeping in mind that there is a time and a place for everything in life which he had grown to understand during his youth some things just cannot be avoided as time would clearly demonstrate that if you stay ready you won't have to get ready.

By 6:00 a.m. every morning he finishes his workout having arrived there at 4:30 a.m. being the first one in when they open at 5:00. Still dressed in black gym attire, gym shoes black hooded sweat shirt now outside in the gold Cadillac driving up Normandy headed towards Inglewood when in his rearview mirror he notices he is being followed but does not recognize the car as having seen it before.

Keeping his distance he makes a number of turns to see if they follow and they do. He pulls into the Shell gas station there on the corner of Vermont and Rosecrans Wearing his face mask he steps out of the car walking towards the door when the car enters the gas station. The blacked out window on the driver's side comes down to reveal a masked hooded driver aiming an automatic pistol at Johnny who through the reflection on the glass he can see when from the clip holster at the lower spine of his back he produces the 38. Just as shots ring out from the black ford.

The glass on the building shatters as he retreats inside from the bullets he kneels taking aim at the figure behind the wheel firing three rounds the car screams away with the driver still firing his weapon indiscriminately a bullet hits the clerk inside between the eyes exiting at the back of his head wrap.

The likelihood of a police car showing up anytime soon was anybody's guess since the police were just as nervous as the general public was so it would take longer to orchestrate enough officers to respond. Broken glass fragments from the window hit Johnny above his left eye blood making it difficult to see out of it.

It was strange the way the police responded when they did arrive. The first thing they did was set up a perimeter behind them protecting their rear opposed to approaching the scene in normal procedure.

This was not by any means normal. The city camera's captured the entire act on video capturing the plate number when the car drove in the station along with security cameras inside. The sound of fire engine sirens off in the distance taken over by the overhead news helicopter flying a safe distance above the police chopper

Through the social media the story went viral. The cell phone in his car began to ring while Johnny was still inside the station now filled with uniformed officer's crime scene investigators taking pictures of the deceased clerk on the chalk lined floor while a paramedic attempts to attend to the cut above his eye.

All the while he has the 38. In the clip holster at his back unnoticed by anyone No one even had the notion to search him or consider him as having any participation in the incident. No need to panic although still he remains cautious of everything going on around him clearly having no idea who could possibly be targeting him and he thought about the lick with the cocaine and if it was possible that some way it was linked back to him, but no. The old P.O. clearly had an axe to grind since the proclaimed Hard Nose met his match when he met Johnny, but would he still attempt to be so bold after being exposed during his first attempt Possible but not likely Maybe it was a Good Ole Boy trying to make his Bones.

Two maybe three hours passed before the paramedic asked Johnny if he was certain he did not need to go to the hospital which he declined and gave notice that he was leaving.

Back inside his car checking his messages first call came from Oakland, Donald Rae. He called back the line came alive

"Man you good?" his friend asked

"Yeah I'm great but the clerk had a bad day"

"Man it's all over face book how they acting up all over the country It's like the wild, Wild west" Donald Rae concluded

"So man you be careful down there"

"You too" the connection dies.

His phone began to blow up with text messages from Clarence Wells Kenny Gales James Burks even Diamond Ken all asking if he was alright when the phone rang again this time its Reba,

"Pop! Are you okay!" she spoke with elevated nervousness

"Yeah I'm good" he replied without hesitation

"Were you hit I could see blood"

"No just flying glass only the clerk caught one"

"How are the kids doing" he asks

"They're good we keep a constant check on each other throughout the day with all this crazy stuff going on that's why I'm calling you" she said with a sigh

"Not to worry I got this and I'll stay in touch" he assured her as the connection went dead. He turned the ignition key to the immediate purr of the engine then sped away towards Compton to the library across from the fast food restaurant. He parked his car near the library and walked across the street. There in the parking lot of the small mini mall was the black ford with three bullet holes in the driver's side door.

He was honestly hoping that his instincts were wrong but there could be no doubt. There were three separate business' in that tiny mall. One of them was owned by his son.

Spots On A Leopard

As the years progressed after being released from federal prison there were several years that he made attempts to establish a relationship with his son, but his son kept attempting to include his mother who even in her demented state of mind would tell people that his father never had the slightest interest in her emotionally while Johnny made it known to his son,

"If it wasn't for marijuana and Crown Royal

you wouldn't even be here" a truth that had scared the boy emotionally scars that he has carried with him all his life while secretly attempting to direct attention on Johnny with the local police through his non-profit community service program, especially since in the year before the boy was born the police department knew him well in a bad way.

When a police officer discovered a girl he was hopeless in love with was

in reality a prostitute like any other Trick he has it in his mind that the pimp is forcing her to do it which is as far from the truth as the Pope is not catholic. But it wasn't until one night after a rendezvous at a local motel despite his desperate pleas to drive her home she refused, but he watched her walk off into the night up the street to get into a black thunderbird. He had the plate ran. It came back John Collier otherwise known by the police as Johnny.

At that time he was fresh out of Soledad State prison on parole after serving ten years to life sentence for eleven counts of armed robbery and three counts of bank robbery over a five year span. Ultimately time brought about a change along the roads of trials and tribulations all created from choices made, good or bad that cannot be undone, long accepting the fact that there was nothing in his past that he could change or alter to any degree outside of creating a Lie, but No.

A philosopher once said

"In order to understand everything you learn to forgive everything" Not Forget! But to let go of the emotional button engaged at the mention of the subject a mechanism that is controlling you

Still his natural instincts would not take on a possibility of attempting a line of communication between them considering the boy's mindset is clear.

He is out for the sake of revenge.

Plainly put, Revenge for being born, the Seed of a man who thought no more about him than he did eliminating his bowels every morning, this created in his own mind while at the same time his true feelings were being conveyed through his actions which Johnny had picked up on from simply watching the boy as he grew into a man. Like the spots on a leopard don't change, neither do the habits of disturbed people who abuse innocent children all for the sake of their warped sense of pleasure.

It made no difference to Johnny that it was his son who had confided in him that he had molested his step daughter when he was married while living in northern California His position on the matter had no room for exceptions other than to distance himself. Not just for his own sake in regards to the law, but he knew that trusting himself not to snatch the life out of his son should he come within arm's reach was uncertain.

For millions of people of all races Family is the one most important thing that matters. Never mind their moral issues displayed on young children too inexperienced to know anything about life are not only against the law but also destroying the life of the child at the same time something that goes beyond his reasoning. In other words why would any grown person who was sexually abused as a child and was injured by it either physically or mentally, chose to inflict that same pain on a child.

What were the chances of that black ford in the parking lot in the mall not having anything to do with his son It could have been stolen then left there. Allowing room for the benefit of doubt still realizing that his instincts have never led him wrong in the past

Still deciding on which mode of action to take walking back to his car he stops and walks back to the shop owned by his son. Patrons have to be buzzed in from the inside after pressing the intercom button on the door There are people inside behind the counter as a voice comes alive

"Hello, Do you have an appointment?"

"No I need to speak with the owner

I'm his father" Johnny speaks calmly as the speaker on the door goes silent. He can still see through the tinted windows to view the people moving about inside. He presses the intercom button again when some unintelligible voice says

"He not here" going silent while Johnny is looking through the glass to watch as the people inside are retreating out of view to the back of the store.

Returning to his car Johnny realizes that clearly his opposition will not be with one person all the while thinking to himself

"I'm too old for this!" But not too weak to stand up and make it known that I am still the same person as always A challenge he would address as the situation called for it. Bringing back a time when his son was sixteen and made a disrespectful comment over the phone to his father Johnny who was not in his son's life at the time, while his son knew the reputation of his father when seeing him again standing on the corner of Compton and El Segundo at the bus stop with a 25. Automatic about to fall out of his pants Johnny got out of his car Snatched the boy up tossing him yelling and screaming into the back of his Stage Coach Cadillac Se Ville and took him to his mother's job at the post office leaving him there with her.

Everything is so much different now. It was like the time has arrived when it is safe show how you really feel and profit from the fabrications at the expense of someone who had no intentions of being a parent of yours or anyone else's from the very beginning so if you know that then what is there to be angry about. Life goes on.

Even though Johnny was acquainted with many people in Los Angeles his association was extremely limited to certain people whom he knew personally were of the same Energy as he. Christopher was one of those people. Somewhere in his late 40's a gambler former neighbor and solid

Early the next Sunday morning he calls Johnny inviting him for a smoke driving his diplomat blue four door custom 150 Now parked in front of the garage Chris shares some news while rolling a blunt,

"Man my brother Von got busted last night for strong arm robbery. I called the station and they told me the charge was two eleven"

"You sure that's what he said because that's worse

That's Armed Robbery" Johnny corrected while Christopher was adamant with his reply

"Yeah that's what he said. Two eleven of the penal code"

"In that case he will be in need of a lawyer because a Public Defender and the District Attorney both get their pay check from the same place so the only thing he's going to do is tell him to make a deal other than that he is penitentiary bound" Johnny concludes shaking his head sadly.

"Where did all this happen" Johnny asked

"Over by the weed spot on Compton below Santa Fe"

The same place where Johnny was when he observed the old PO dressed like a ninja attempting to play him out of his car so he could be shot to death. But simply by paying attention prevented him from being on the evening news His cell phone rings it's one of his sisters from up north,

"What's up Gina" Johnny asks his younger sister Regina

"Johnny, Raymond is dead. He was shot at a police rally in Vallejo"

Raymond, his oldest brother who was assigned as a special investigator to the district attorney of Solano County While attending a political fund raiser for an election when a group of heavily armed men stormed the building killing seven wounding nine His brother was the first shot. Johnny was seriously at a loss for words. Not out of sadness but out of not feeling anything at all replying,

"No shit! Seriously Damn" There was never any sense of Family or even of brotherhood between them. Although he was sad to learn of his younger brother Russell passing a few years earlier due to hospital error since the two always saw eye to eye and respected each other without judgement but other than that, that was all there was to it leaving him searching for something to say,

"Well, with all this COVID restrictions going on I doubt if I attend the service unless its on Zoom"

Johnny concludes letting her know he was in the middle of something and had to go.

"Okay" she replied

"I'll send you a text to let you know about the service" and the call drops.

Later that evening it was on the news that the car sought after in the gas station shooting was located in the parking lot of a small mini mart in Compton with three bullet holes in the driver's side door Inside the car was recovered a 38. Police revolver with the serial numbers still visible Traced the gun being stolen from the home of a Vacaville detective and used in a murder

From the surveillance camera's Johnny can be clearly seen firing his weapon at the black ford something the police had missed in their fear of being played into a surprise attack but now have more questions to ask him. When a call comes in on his caller ID as LAPD he allows it to go to voice mail. A detective asking him to come in But as he is re-enacting that day back tracking the events Surely by now there has been a closer look at the camera's showing his part in the foray

Although he was no longer on any type of parole or supervision he still would not willingly accept an invitation from the police to come in for a visit. Having past experience with previous request without a lawyer is not advisable, while altering his life to focus on events that can only lead to a legal complication lawyer fees and possible bail money, so if the invite was that important get a warrant.

His two classic Cadillac's stood out in the streets along with both being registered and insured in his name, while the SUV was leased under the name of a woman who works at the dealership, a Soccer Mom looking type vehicle silver gray in color unsuspecting with handicap plates' he drove without being concerned of being pulled over.

Beneath the spare tire in the back was the kilo of cocaine he had taken from the coin store robbery. The product was good, so good in fact that he had to sample it to be sure urging him to hurry up and sell it before he had too much of a sample and ended up a victim of his own demise

"Ant" was into Flipping Car's from his home on 118 th in Compton. At one point he was in the drug game selling large quantities of a drug called "Wet Daddy's" by the gallons earning him millions. But it took one too many attempts on his life from being shot and robed to influence him to get out of the dope game and into the car restoration game. He still enjoyed good Blow which was becoming more difficult to obtain good quality causing the prices to sky rocket.

Johnny had known Ant for a number of years, in fact Johnny bought the gold 77 Se Ville from Ant and was now taking the cocaine to him to sell knowing full and well that Ant also liked young girls and chances are he would use most of it for his own purpose so he was making it a gift no strings attached.

Just as Johnny is about to leave Ant remembers

"Oh yeah I saw your boy who sent this guy to me asking to buy a car I was selling he still owes me two hundred I did it because it was your boy"

"What kind of car was it" Johnny asked

"A bucket a black ford" Ant answered

"Yeah well I don't associate with that clown so-"

"No I wasn't asking you to do anything I was just mentioning it"

"Text him and just blow up his phone" Johnny suggested

"He'll answer after a bit"

That answers the question of who those people were at the store owned by his son that day or at least one of them. Clearly a sign that the issues his son has with him have gone beyond any form of mending but to a life or death situation stemmed solely from the fear his son has of his father exposing him as a pedophile while the truth of it Johnny found humiliating and embarrassing his reason for distancing himself

The way Johnny had it figured no matter what he did from this point on with his own life would be judged by people no matter what and the only thing he knew how to do was be himself What other people do who share the same last name has nothing to do with him especially after he has gone from the Planet then what difference does it make.

One thing was for certain, No one gets out of this life alive...

50 Feet

The concept of Social Distancing has always been an ideal that Johnny created except he required forty-four more feet than required. He was not one into what he called "Buddy Hustling" The more so called friends you had the more likely you were to be called upon to assist in some problem that has absolutely nothing to do with anything that makes sense. Sucker ducking for the most part....

Epilogue

The story though Fiction is based on real life events involving real people with issues like so many thousands of other people have but dare not speak of out loud for the sake of keeping the peace or what excuse they employ to justify the logic. Most times it turns out to be Blame when in truth it is nothing but Choice.

A philosopher once said, "We choose our misery and sorrow long before we experience them". To fully understand this principal one has to be open for mental growth and change or be like stagnant water and breed nothing but reptiles of the mind

In other words, the one Hero in your life starts with You.

About The Author

Born July 20,1950 in Chicago, Ill. Relocated to the San Francisco Bay area in 1964.

2021

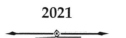

"You can't miss what you never had" Easily stated from an individual point of view But I find myself thinking about all of the nieces nephews and grandchildren I will not ever have the opportunity to share with due to an understanding that can be as lethal as COVID 19 Not for me because I have always known how to keep my distance

I made the choice to live my life destructively many years ago with no room for excuses or Buck Passing.

Printed in the United States
By Bookmasters